VENGEANCE BE HANGED!

"You've got a lot more land than anybody's got a right to!" Barstow exploded.

"That's where you're wrong," Jessie replied.

Barstow had his mouth open to reply when his eyes fell on the two dead men lashed to the horse. "You killed some of my men to boot! One of my best hands and one of the Galvanized Yankees! And that's something I'll sure make you pay for!"

"I'm afraid you've got your ideas turned backward," Jessie said coolly. Turning to Ki, she went on. "Cut the rope . . ."

★   ★   ★   ★   ★

Turn to the back for an exciting preview of a new Western epic . . .

RIVERBOAT
by Douglas Hirt

First in a series about the adventures of the men and women who struggled to survive and prosper in the golden age of the Mississippi.

◆ WESLEY ELLIS ◆

LONE STAR

AND THE
GALVANIZED YANKEES

J
JOVE BOOKS, NEW YORK

LONE STAR AND THE GALVANIZED YANKEES

A Jove Book / published by arrangement with
the author

PRINTING HISTORY
Jove edition / February 1995

ISBN: 0-515-11552-5

A JOVE BOOK®
Jove Books are published by The Berkley Publishing Group,
200 Madison Avenue, New York, New York 10016.
JOVE and the "J" design are trademarks
belonging to Jove Publications, Inc.

PRINTED IN THE UNITED STATES OF AMERICA

10 9 8 7 6 5 4 3 2 1

LONE STAR

AND THE
GALVANIZED YANKEES

★
Chapter 1

"Stay on my right side!" Jessie called to Ki as she glanced at the four riders galloping away and gestured toward them. Ki nodded and reined away from her as he spurred his mount to a gallop.

Jessie measured with her eyes the distance that separated them from the fleeing horsemen and continued. "I'll angle to the left! When we get within range we'll have them between us!"

Ki acknowledged her call with a wave of his hand, and drummed his heels on his horse's sides to speed the animal's advance. Jessie had already reined ahead of him. She'd urged Sun to a gallop and the magnificent palomino was moving at its fastest pace.

Scanning the terrain between himself and the escaping horsemen, Ki saw that he was not quite

1

as close as Jessie was to the men they'd surprised. Both he and Jessie had needed only one quick glance to realize that the four men now galloping away were rustlers who'd invaded the Circle Star range in search of cattle that would be easy to steal.

Jessie and Ki had spurred ahead when they'd seen the rustlers. The cattle thieves had seen Jessie and Ki first and had already begun to gallop away, abandoning the small bunch of steers they'd been herding up before driving them off the Circle Star range. The renegades had not even made an effort to attack, even though all had rifles in their saddle scabbards.

Now Jessie slid her rifle from its dangling scabbard and took quick aim on the farthest rustler. Her lead flew true. The outlaw sagged in his saddle. His rifle dropped from his hands as he lurched forward. His horse began bucking wildly when the falling weapon struck one of its hind legs.

For a moment the dead man stretched slumped down atop his saddlehorn. Then he began slipping slowly to one side and fell to the ground, landing in a limp heap. Without a rider to guide him, the outlaw's horse started walking slowly away from the prone form.

"If we want to catch up with the others, we'll have some hard riding to do," Jessie called as Ki started toward her.

"You mean to let them get away?" he asked.

"Not if we can help it," she called back after a quick glance around the area ahead.

"Then we'd better spur up," Ki said. "I don't think they'll be able to hold a gallop very long, and our horses are still fresh. We can beat their pace easily enough to stay in range."

"What I'm thinking is that they might've reined into that gully yonder and are just waiting for us to show ourselves when we get to the top of that long rise," Jessie said.

"Let's slant off toward the low spot over to our left," she went on. "We don't know which way they rode after we lost sight of them, and we don't want to get caught in an ambush."

"We sure don't," Ki agreed. "But we don't have much choice but to keep after them."

Jessie did not reply, but nodded without taking her eyes off the crest of the long upslope. The distance they had to cover was not great, but the steep upslope slowed the pace of their mounts. At last they topped the rim of the rise and saw the outlaws ahead. The men had separated and gained space between themselves and Jessie and Ki. None of the outlaws were within certain range, even for rifles.

Neither Jessie nor Ki wasted ammunition. They did not reply to the few scattered shots let off by the fleeing rustlers after the men ahead had seen them. But they pressed on, trying to get close enough for their shots to be fully effective. Then, suddenly, the rustlers vanished as quickly as if some magician had waved his wand over their quarry.

"There's a drop-off ahead if I remember rightly," Jessie called to Ki. "And too many small canyons to count beyond it. I hate to give up, but it's a pretty sure bet that the rustlers will split up."

"I can't argue about that," Ki agreed. "And by now I don't think we've got a chance of catching up with them."

Jessie pulled up. "So let's cut our losses and get back to that little herd of steers those rustlers were trying to steal. We'd better bunch them before we leave."

"Suppose you ride back to the main house and bring back two or three of the hands," Ki suggested. "I'll stay on the trail of those rustlers and mark my trail so you can catch up with me."

Jessie shook her head. "By the time I get back here, it'll be too dark to follow even a marked trail. Little as I like the idea of letting those scoundrels get off free, I think we'd better just have Ed send a couple of the hands out here and drive the cattle to a range closer to the main house."

"Suppose I just stay here and keep an eye on this part of the range until we get those hands out here," Ki said.

"I don't think we need to worry about the rustlers," Jessie replied, frowning as she glanced at the declining sun. She shook her head. "The way the rustlers were running, they're not likely to stop. They'll be thinking like we have, that from now on some of the hands will be on guard out here."

"Then we'd better bunch these steers and drive them closer to the fence line," Ki suggested.

"I'll work from the left and you go right," Jessie said. "We'll need to make a short job of gathering. In case you've forgotten about Dave Barry's wire, he's supposed to be here today or tomorrow. I don't know exactly what he has in mind, but he wouldn't be coming all this distance unless he thought it was important. I'd like to be at the main house to greet him when he gets here."

"Dave's a really solid man," Ki said. "But if we're going to get back to the main house any-time soon, we'd better get busy with our hazing."

Jessie nodded as she wheeled Sun around. Ki reined in the opposite direction, and they set about their task of gathering the scattered steers.

"Now that we've finished supper, suppose we take our coffee into the big room where we'll be more comfortable," Jessie suggested that evening.

She glanced from David Barry to Ki as she stood up. They were pushing their chairs away from the table and reaching for their coffee cups. Turning, Jessie led them into the expansive chamber which was not only the center of the Circle Star's main house, but the heart of most of its activities.

Lamps had already been lighted in what Jessie

called the big room. It was as large as three rooms in a house of average size. Leather-upholstered divans faced each other in its center, and several easy chairs were scattered around them. On the walls two large oil portraits dominated the big chamber. One was of Jessie's mother, who'd died giving birth to her. The other portrayed Jessie's father, Alex Starbuck, the financial genius who had created an empire during his all-too-short life.

Jessie waited for Barry and Ki to choose seats, then sat down on the divan that faced both men. She turned to Barry and said, "Now suppose you tell us about this furniture factory that's going to be put up for sale, Dave. I'm not saying that I'm interested in buying it, but from the little bit you mentioned in your telegram, I just might be."

"Well, the main thing which occurred to me is that it's so close to the mill you now own in Davenport that buying it can save you a lot of time and money," Barry declared.

"You know that's something I'm always interested in doing." Jessie smiled. "So go ahead and fill me in."

"First of all, the factory's in good condition," Barry said. "It's been closed for almost two years, but it wouldn't be a big job or cost a great deal to get it into operation again. The next thing is that the place has been closed for such a long time that the stockholders are impatient. They want action, and they're not getting any."

"You're saying that they want a sale very quickly," Jessie said thoughtfully.

"Exactly," Barry replied. "And I'm pretty well satisfied that if you made a firm offer, complete with earnest money, you could save a great deal and make it a much more efficient operation. In a very short time your increased profits will more than pay for it."

Jessie sat silently for a moment, then nodded. "There's no need for you to show me figures right now, Dave. I'm sure you have them ready, and I'm equally sure that they're accurate."

"You've done enough business through my office to know that, Jessie," Barry said. "And I've learned that any decision you make will be a good one."

"It's nice to be appreciated." Jessie smiled again. "But I'm not going to give you an answer right this minute."

Barry nodded. "There's no real hurry, not unless someone else gets wind of the fact that the mill's on the market. I've tried to keep things as quiet as possible, to give you the first chance at it."

"I appreciate your work, Dave," Jessie said. "At least give me the night to think it over. I'll look at your figures in the morning."

Suddenly a short series of raps on the main house door reached their ears.

Ki had started to get up after the first knock. He said, "You and David go on with your talk.

7

That's probably Ed Wright. I'll go let him in."

As Ki started for the door, Jessie said to Barry, "I don't know about you, but my coffee cup needs filling. Suppose I take yours as well and fill it while I'm tending to mine."

"A very good idea," Barry agreed. "But I'll go with you if I can be of any help."

"It's just a step," Jessie replied as she stood up. "But if you want to stretch your legs a bit, this is as good a chance as any."

Barry smiled. "Both the coffee and the leg stretch will do us good."

Then Ki returned, accompanied by Ed Wright. Jessie said to Wright, "Do we have trouble somewhere on the spread, Ed?"

"I hate to say this, but I'm just afraid we do, Miss Jessie," Wright replied. "Not the kind of trouble that means we'll have to be doing something now, but I figured you'd better hear about it tonight instead of waiting till morning."

"Then come sit down and tell me about it," she said.

Barry broke in. "I don't want to be in the way, Jessie. Suppose I just excuse myself and go up to bed."

"You won't be in the way at all, Dave," Jessie told him. "But I know you've had a very long train trip, and I'm sure that what Ed's got on his mind doesn't have anything to do with furniture factories."

After Barry had left, Jessie turned to Wright.

"Well, what's the problem, Ed? Let's get fresh coffee and talk."

"You two sit down and I'll bring the coffee," Ki volunteered. "If I miss anything while I'm away, you can fill me in when I get back."

After Jessie and Wright had settled down, she said, "Well, Ed?"

"Well, Jessie, I might be seeing ghosts under the bed," he began. "But I'm worried about what I think is happening on the northeast range."

"You should be able to handle cattle problems without coming to me, Ed."

Before Wright could reply, Ki came in with a coffeepot and cups on a tray. He took advantage of the silence that had followed Jessie's reply to Wright to place filled cups within their reach, and was moving toward a chair for himself when the foreman replied.

"It's not the cattle, Jessie," Wright said. "It's the squatters."

"What squatters, Ed? Have I been missing something?"

Wright shook his head. "If you've missed anything, I have too. But these problems are something we haven't faced before. I didn't find out myself about them until Joe Avery came in from riding fence, just after dark."

"Then go ahead and tell Ki and me what's wrong," Jessie suggested.

"I'm trying to figure out where to begin," Wright replied. A small twisted frown had formed on his bronzed face. "And I don't have anything to go by except what Joe Avery told me."

"Joe's reliable," Ki stated. "I've ridden range and herded steers with him. What is it he's run into?"

"Joe's been riding boundary fence these past three days," Wright explained. "There's a bunch of people up on the northeast stretch of the Circle Star, Jessie. Mostly men, just a few women, from what Joe said. And what he told me is that they're planning to start a town there."

For a moment all that Jessie could do was to stare at the foreman. Then she said, "How could anybody be stupid enough to try a thing like that? That land's fenced, so they certainly must know they're on the Circle Star range."

"Oh, sure," Wright agreed. "They know that, Jessie. And it doesn't seem to bother them in the least."

"Don't they realize they'll be building on land that doesn't belong to them?" Jessie asked.

"Of course they do. But even knowing they're on Circle Star range, they had the nerve to tell Joe that the land they're claiming for themselves is open for settlement by whoever claims it."

Jessie sat in silence. At last she asked, "Did Joe get any hint from what they said how they expect to get away with such a silly move?"

"Nothing except what I just told you, that gibberish about idle land belonging to whoever claimed it."

"But that's not idle land!" Jessie exclaimed. "It belongs to the Circle Star and has for years! Alex was too shrewd a businessman to tolerate even a small flaw in the deeds to any land he bought. Did Joe tell you anything else about the run-in he had with the squatters?"

"He didn't say anything I haven't mentioned except that one of them told him these folks call themselves Galvanized Yankees."

"I've heard the phrase before," Jessie said. "But that's neither here nor there. I can understand why Joe didn't want to press too hard and very likely get into a fight when he was outnumbered."

"That's about the way I looked at it," Wright agreed. "And I don't think he knows much about how your father put the Circle Star together. But the squatters are there and from what Joe gathered they're all set to build houses—I'd guess more shacks than houses—on your range."

Jessie was silent for a moment. Then she said, "I'll have to admit that I can't come up with anything right this minute, Ed. But you be sure to sit down with Joe Avery as soon as you can manage and go over everything he knows about the squatters. Then we'll put our heads together at breakfast tomorrow and see what we can do to stop those land thieves."

★

Chapter 2

Jessie did not stop on the way to her room, but as she passed Dave Barry's door she tapped at it lightly with her fingertips. As soon as she closed her own bedroom door she took off her skirt and blouse. She was slipping her chemise over her head when the light sound of fingertips tapping at her own door broke the room's silence. Letting the flimsy garment fall to the floor as she moved, Jessie went to the door and opened it a crack, then swung it fully open to admit her caller.

"I was beginning to think you and Ki were going to take up the rest of the night making plans," Barry said as he stepped into the room.

"You're too impatient," Jessie replied, shutting the door behind him. "I knew you were waiting for my signal, and I got away as soon as I could."

"None of that matters now that you're here." Barry smiled. "We've got a lot of lost time to make up."

He was draped in a dressing gown, and now he shrugged it off his shoulders. His erection was just beginning as he stood naked and held out his arms to Jessie. She was already moving toward him. Barry locked his arms around her and she tilted her head back for his kiss. They stood in their embrace for a moment, tongues entwining, before Barry tightened his arms around her. Without breaking their kiss, he lifted her and stepped to the side of her bed.

"Wait just a moment," Jessie said, breaking their kiss at last.

Even before she stopped speaking she was groping at Barry's crotch to place him. Then she locked her legs around him and whispered, "Now!"

Barry leaned forward and Jessie tightened the muscles of her legs to pull him into her as they toppled to the bed. While she was dropping backward Jessie relaxed the grip of her thighs to let Barry's weight complete his penetration. He drove fully into her, and a sharp ecstatic cry broke from her lips.

Neither of them spoke. When Barry started stroking, Jessie began to twist her hips while gasps of pleasure escaped from her lips. Barry kept stroking lustily, long regular lunges, and now Jessie's gasps changed to short-lived throaty cries as each of his thrusts ended with the impact of their bodies. Jessie's arms were around him now, and she tightened her embrace each time one of his lusty penetrations ended.

Barry paced his thrusting, holding himself buried fully at the culmination of each lunge, and each time as he pressed against her Jessie rotated her hips for a few moments. Then she relaxed the embrace of her legs in a silent invitation for him to drive again. Barry understood her move. He began driving in slow, measured thrusts, and as the minutes ticked off he waited less and less between his strokes.

Jessie began moaning happily, a succession of throaty happy sighs in response to her lover's deep drives. She started to twist her hips as his stroking continued and Barry showed no sign of stopping. Soon Jessie's soft moans sharpened in tone, breaking the room's silence at shorter and still shorter intervals.

Now Barry sought Jessie's lips with his. As their lips met and their tongues entwined, he increased the tempo of his lusty thrusts. He drove in a rhythm that matched the tempo of Jessie's gyrating hips. Soon her soft moans became a constant susurrus of happy gasps, while Jessie twisted her hips in a tempo that matched the steady rhythmic penetration of Barry's lunges.

As the moments passed, Jessie's moans of pleasure formed into a continuing cry. The cry was a short one, but it was followed by another longer and louder moan. Her body began to tremble in quick sweeping jerks, which culminated in a frantic writhing accompanied by a burst of throbbing gasps. Then there was a moment of frantic movement as both Jessie and Barry jerked and shuddered into the ultimate peak of shared fulfillment.

Moments ticked away before their small gasps faded as their heaving bodies stilled and they lay quiet. Both Jessie and Barry were limp, and remained motionless while their breathing slowly returned to its normal tempo. At last Jessie spoke.

"Let's don't move for a while," she whispered. "I like the feel of having you in me."

"If you'd like to lie still, I'd be the last man in the world to disturb you," Barry told her. "Just tell me if I feel too heavy."

"That time will never come," she replied. "But you tell me when you're ready to start again, and I'll be ready for you. This night won't last forever, and I know you've got to leave after breakfast tomorrow morning to catch your train. I want to stretch the darkness as long as possible."

"Then that's what we'll do," he promised. "And if you're thinking I'm too tired, I'm ready to start again if you are."

"I was hoping that's what you'd say," Jessie replied. "And the best time that I can think of to start over is right now."

• • •

"I was sure that Ed would be here before now," Jessie said as she and Ki pushed away from the breakfast table and stood up. "When I went with David to the corral to see him off, Ed was there. He was sorting out the range riders, seeing that they had their day's work lined out. And I suppose he's still down there."

"More than likely," Ki agreed. "He'll show up in a few minutes, though. I have an idea he's—" Ki broke off as a knock sounded from the door. "Likely that's Ed now. I'll go let him in. I suppose you'll want to go in the main room to talk?"

"Why don't you bring him in here," Jessie suggested. "I'll put out a cup and saucer for him and we can sit here at the table."

Ki nodded and started for the door while Jessie went to the wall cupboard and took out a cup and saucer. She carried them to the table and looked in the oversized coffeepot to make sure there was enough for the three of them. By the time she'd filled all three cups Ki had returned with the Circle Star foreman.

"I'm sorry I'm so late getting here, Jessie," Wright said as he and Ki entered the room. "I had to go over with Joe Avery what he'd told me about those squatters. It took me longer than I'd figured."

"You're planning to have Joe go with us, of course," Jessie said.

"I was pretty sure that's what you'd want me to do," Wright said. "And I've already told him to be ready to ride when we leave. He knows exactly where the squatters are."

"And you cautioned the fence riders to steer clear of them until we have some sort of plan?" Jessie asked.

"Oh, I wouldn't overlook something like that," Wright replied. "The less they have to do with squatters, the better it'll be. You know that if they run across strangers who don't have any business, there's a pretty fair chance they'd stir up a fracas."

"You're right, of course," Jessie agreed. "But rather than sit here and talk, maybe we'd best finish our coffee and get started."

A few minutes later, as they moved toward the doorway, Wright said, "I've told a few of our men to stay close to the main house in case you want them to go with us."

"I think you and Joe will be enough," Jessie said quickly. "Just keep in mind the old saying about honey catching more flies than vinegar. Ki and I talked for a few minutes last night, trying to figure out the best way to approach them."

"And what did you come up with?" Wright asked.

"We can talk about that while we're on the way to the squatters," Jessie said. "It's a long ride to the boundary fence, and we don't need to be in any sort of hurry."

They'd reached the hitch rail outside the main

house by now. Joe Avery was standing at the rail, where Sun—Jessie's golden palomino—and three workhorses were tethered. After hellos were exchanged, they broke off conversation while they mounted.

Once they were in their saddles Jessie took the lead. They rode single file and in silence until they'd zigzagged beyond the last of the sprawling ranch's outbuildings. Now, with the open prairie stretching ahead, Jessie turned in her saddle and signaled for the others to ride closer to her.

Ki reached Jessie's side first. He was followed at once by Wright and Joe Avery. They reined into a rough line that brought them into speaking distance, with Jessie and Ki flanked by Wright and Avery. Jessie touched Sun's reins to keep his gait to a slow walk.

"We've got a sizeable stretch to cover to get to the squatters," she said to her companions. "Maybe Joe could ride next to me and tell me exactly what happened when he ran across those people yesterday."

"He's the one that's got the most talking to do, I guess," Wright agreed. "Suppose I ride on Ki's off-side and Joe can traipse along at your on-side."

"That's workable," Jessie agreed, and Wright and Avery switched places.

"If you don't mind me saying so, Miss Jessie," Avery began, "that outfit I run into yesterday was mostly hard cases. And it didn't take me long to find out they're the kind that goes stomping around looking for trouble."

"I'd like to keep everything peaceful with that bunch," Jessie declared. "But we certainly won't run from trouble if they start any sort of fracas. Though I'd like to avoid anything like a showdown, even if they prove to be unreasonable."

"Like I told Ed, that bunch ain't much better'n outlaws, Miss Jessie."

"And you really think all of them are like that?" Jessie asked.

"Oh, sure," Avery said. "Even the women looked like they was the kind that some folks call *barbados*."

Jessie frowned. "How many women are there?"

Avery hesitated for a moment before replying. "Why, I couldn't rightly say, Miss Jessie. I reckon I seen five or six, but I figure there might be more. Trouble was, I couldn't always tell 'em from the men right off."

"And how many men?"

"Hard to say. Maybe twenty or so."

"Were they all carrying guns, even the women?" she asked.

"I can't say that all of them was," Avery replied. "But most of 'em seemed to be."

Jessie rode in silence for a moment. Then she asked, "Have they started to put up any sort of buildings yet?"

"Not a one," Avery answered. "And I didn't see

no stacks of boards anyplace around. But there was one big tent they was starting to lay out flat so's they could pitch it."

Ki had been listening to the conversation between Jessie and Avery. As Avery finished replying to Jessie's question he broke in. "I imagine you saw bedrolls all over the place then?"

"Oh, sure, Ki," Avery replied. "Some of 'em in bunches and some of 'em scattered out."

"I suppose there are a lot of wagons, too," Jessie said. "And horses?"

"There ain't as many wagons as you might think, Miss Jessie," Avery replied. "Maybe six or eight. But there was a real good bunch of horses and mules in a rope corral."

"That outfit can't've been there very long, then," Jessie said. She turned to Wright and asked, "Do you remember the last time one of our hands rode over that range?"

"I wish I could give you a good answer, Miss Jessie," he said. "We don't have any steers on that little section right now, haven't had any for maybe three months, as I recall. It's hard to get to, it's not top graze, and it's not big enough for a real herd."

"It's a right pesky stretch of graze," Jessie agreed. "Too big to let go of and not big enough to be of much use. But it's part of the Circle Star, the last piece of range that Alex bought when he was putting the ranch together. That's the main reason why I hold on to it."

21

Ki suddenly spurred a bit ahead of the other riders. Then he wheeled his mount and slapped the reins over its neck, urging it back.

"Jessie!" he called. "If we're going to make any plans about what we'll do when we get to the squatters, we'd better pull up right here! I just got a glimpse of a rider dropping behind this rise we're on!"

"Did he see you and act like he was trying to get away?" Jessie asked.

"I suppose he did, but I can't be sure," Ki told her. "There might've been another man with him. I couldn't see past the rim of that ridge. But it means we're getting close to the squatters. Hadn't we better rein in and make some kind of plan about what you intend for us to do?"

"I've only got one plan, and it's the same one I had when we started out," Jessie replied. Her voice was level and thoughtful. "We're going to convince those squatters that this isn't land open to settlement and if they've got any ideas about starting a new town they'll have to find another place, land that doesn't belong to the Circle Star."

"Suppose they won't listen to you," Ki said.

Jessie did not reply at once. She was eyeing the low ridge ahead that hid the stretch of open grazing land on its other side. At last she said, "I've been asking myself that question almost from the time we heard about the squatters and the plans they have to build a town on Circle Star range, Ki."

When Jessie fell silent, Ki waited for her to continue. Again she did not speak for several moments. Then she went on, her words coming slowly but firmly. "I still haven't come up with an answer that satisfies me. We'll just have to wait and see what they say when I tell them. When we've gotten their answer, we can make our own plans about what to do."

Ki knew Jessie well, and he realized that her answer was one that might have come from her father. He wasted no time in arguing, but simply reined his mount as Jessie toed Sun into motion. Then he nudged the flank of his own mount to follow her.

Ed Wright toed his horse forward, and the little group moved on up the long slant that stretched ahead. The bright Texas sun was still hanging fairly low in the sky, and even on a low rise the wide brims of the hats they wore couldn't keep it from flooding the lower part of their faces.

"I suppose we ought've started later," Jessie told Ki. "It didn't occur to me that we'd be bothered by the sun this time in the morning. But I'd rather have the sun in my face than feel raindrops splashing on it."

"We'll be veering off to the west in a little while," Ki reminded her. "Then we won't have to squint like this."

"And it can't be too soon to suit me," Jessie said. "I think I'd—"

She broke off as a bullet whistled above their

23

heads and raised a puff of dust as it dug into the prairie behind them. Even before the whine of the shell died away Jessie was reaching for the Winchester in her saddle scabbard and Ki was standing up in his stirrups, his rife in his hand, scanning the terrain ahead.

So were Wright and Avery. Like Jessie and Ki, they'd drawn their rifles from their saddle scabbards and were searching the upslope ahead.

"Spread, fast!" Wright called.

He and Joe Avery were already reining away to flank Jessie and Ki. Raising his voice, Wright called, "Jessie, did you or Ki see any gunsmoke from that rifle shot?"

"I didn't," Ki replied.

"And neither did I," Jessie said. "All we can do is ride zigzags until we top this rise. Then maybe we'll get a look at whoever was doing the shooting!"

Chapter 3

Jessie and her companions in the little group were expecting more rifle shots from the low ridge. While zigzagging slowly up the slope all of them kept their eyes busy searching the ridge crest. In spite of their vigilance they saw no signs of movement anywhere along the jagged rise, and there were no more shots fired. When they were still far enough from the crest to be invisible from its opposite side, Jessie signaled for them to halt.

"I've got a pretty good idea that someone in that squatters' outfit fired that shot," Jessie said. "And he might still be around, waiting for us to be better targets. Let's be careful not to show ourselves above the rim of that ridge until we've scouted it for a few minutes."

"I suppose we've all been thinking the same thing," Ki agreed. "Even if there isn't anybody in sight, those shots must've come from somebody in the bunch we're heading for."

"And they're as hard a bunch as any I'd ever hope to see," Avery put in. "There ain't much they'd do that'd surprise me."

Jessie nodded. "But before we start making plans, we'd better take a look at them. It's the only way we've got to figure out what kind of plan we need."

"If you don't object, Jessie, I'll do the looking," Ki volunteered. "I can use *ninjutsu* if I need to, so the squatters down there won't see me."

"Go ahead, Ki," Jessie said. "But I'd say what we're interested in right now is whether there are any signs that the squatters are getting ready to start a fight of some kind."

Ki dismounted and started up the rise. After he'd covered several yards he flattened himself belly-down on the ground and pushed himself forward, on a slant up the slope. When he reached the crest of the ridge he swiveled his head from side to side for several moments inspecting the activities of the group that was in the bottom of the depression. Then he squirmed backward for a few feet before standing up and trotting back to where Jessie and the other two men were waiting.

"There's a lot of people down there, Jessie," Ki reported. "You said the main thing we're interested in right now is whether or not they look peaceful, and I didn't see anything that gave me the idea they were getting ready to do any fighting."

"Well, that's good news," Jessie said. Then she asked, "Did you see any signs that they're getting ready to put up houses or buildings?"

Ki shook his head. "As far as I could tell, they're just milling around. I didn't see any lumber of any kind. What catches your eye first is the great big circus tent they've spread out to pitch on one side of that section of range."

"A circus tent?" Jessie asked.

"That's about the best way I could describe it," Ki said. "One of those big oval tents like you've seen at a circus."

"But that's surely not the only tent you saw," Jessie said.

"Oh, there are plenty of others, a lot of little shelter tents like the cavalrymen in the army carry," Ki answered. "I didn't take time to count them. And there were some wall tents big enough to hold six or eight or people with a little crowding. I'd say there were maybe eight or ten or maybe even a dozen of them. And there were some bedrolls scattered around."

"That sounds to me like they're settling in, Ki."

"It certainly does. I'd imagine that the big tent is likely meant to be a mess hall when they get it raised. And at a guess, most of the other ones are for anybody who might not have anyplace else to sleep. But I got another idea too when I saw them."

"What was it?"

"It occurred to me there's a chance that the big tent might have lumber under it, Jessie. Didn't Joe say that the squatters are planning to build a town?"

"And the town would be on Circle Star range unless they move on!" Jessie exclaimed. "Ki, I don't intend to give them a chance to build on rangeland that my father bought and that I own."

"Well," Ki said thoughtfully, "there's only one way to find out, Jessie."

"Do you think it's safe for us to move ahead, then?" Jessie asked.

"As safe as it'll ever be. But just in case I didn't make the right guess, suppose I start down there by myself. It's the best way I can think of to find out what kind of reception we're likely to get."

"From what you've said, Ki, I don't think we'll need any advance guard," Jessie replied. "And as long as you're pretty sure it's safe, we'll go down there for a closer look. But there's one thing I'm curious about."

"What's that?" Ki frowned.

"You suggested that we go on and push ahead," Jessie told him. "But now I'm not sure how we ought to act. Are we going to be friends of the squatters, or enemies?"

"I certainly don't feel very friendly," Ki replied. "And I'm sure that you don't, either. But you know how I feel about coppering a bet."

"Go ahead," Jessie said. "I'm listening."

"If you recall, this hump runs fairly straight for something more than a mile," Ki replied. "And I'd imagine you're thinking about like I am."

"Probably so," she agreed. "Go on."

"What I'm getting at is that it'd be wise for me to go back to that hump where I was. I can take cover and watch you and the others while you're riding down there."

"And be our ace in the hole if trouble starts?" Jessie asked. Ki nodded and she went on. "I'll agree that it's a good idea. For all we know right now, they might be getting ready to attack the Circle Star."

"Why'd they want to do that, Miss Jessie?" Avery asked. "We haven't choused them around or made trouble for them. Not yet, anyways."

"You've heard about the Barbary pirates, haven't you?" she asked him.

"I don't know much about them except their name," Avery replied. "But they was ocean sailors, not range riders."

"Of course," Jessie agreed. "I mentioned them because of what history tells us. The pirates had a trick of getting their own way by capturing somebody who was important and threatening to kill them unless they got ransom money."

"But they . . ." Avery began. Then the puzzled frown that had grown on his face vanished. "I see what you mean now, Miss Jessie. The squatters might figure that if they got hold of Ed or me or somebody else from the Circle Star, they'd say to you that they'd turn us loose if you'd give 'em the land they want for their town."

"That's the general idea," Ki put in. "It'd be easier for them to pull a trick like that instead of fighting."

"Of course," Jessie said. "But we're wasting time doing all this talking. We've come here to warn those people there'll be trouble if they start trying to build a town on Circle Star range, and right now's the time to get down to brass tacks."

"I only need a few minutes," Ki assured her.

He nodded and reined away from the little group. They watched him as he rode along the slope of the rise until he'd reached the rock formation that was to be his shelter. Taking his Winchester from its saddle scabbard, Ki dismounted and waved to his companions. Then he took two steps and disappeared into the outcrop of stone.

"We'll give him a minute to get settled," Jessie told Ed Wright and Avery. "Then we'll start out. Remember, we won't take our rifles out of their scabbards unless we need them. I want this visit to be a sensible discussion, not a gunfight."

Wright and Avery nodded.

After a minute or so they all nudged their horses ahead. Jessie rode in the lead and when they'd passed the rock outcrop that had been their cover and the depression on the ground below came into view, she reined in and turned to her companions.

"When we get to where we can see all that stretch of ground where the squatters have pitched camp, we'd better stop just long enough to get a good look at them," she said. "From here we can see almost the whole little valley, and I don't mind admitting that I don't like what I see."

What the Circle Star trio saw was that the little depression they were looking at seemed alive with people. There were not any really large bunches visible, but in several places little groups of three or four, and a few as large as a half-dozen, were standing talking. There were two or three patches of open ground where bedrolls dotted the ground, and near the center, groups of small two-man army tents dotted the level terrain.

They saw several groups of men working around the edges of a large tent which had been spread flat on the ground. The workers were examining lengths of rope and driving in long pegs around the perimeter of the tent walls, and following them were other men busy cutting long sections off the lengths of rope and attaching them to the ends of the tent poles.

At some little distance from the tents other men were working at rope corrals that enclosed a number of horses. A few untethered horses and mules were grazing or ambling idly around in the low depression. Several men with shovels in their hands were scooping dirt from a sizeable area which was covered with a dense growth of tall green prairie grass.

Close to them, three men were standing in a triangle. From time to time one would point to or gesticulate at the area of dense grass, then turn back to continue the harangue that was obviously aimed at his two companions. Just beyond the spot where the trio stood there was a larger group of men, all of them holding or leaning on shovels.

Even at a distance it was easy to see that they were getting ready to begin digging, but as yet they'd made no move toward doing so. Their attention was fixed on that trio, which stood a small distance apart, having some sort of discussion.

Jessie completed her quick survey of their immediate surroundings. Then she returned her full attention to the large bunch of men carrying shovels and the smaller group engaged in a discussion. She gestured toward the three men, who were still arguing. Touching her boot toe to Sun's flank, she reined the big stallion toward them, and her companions followed.

"It looks to me as though these squatters are really going to try to build on Circle Star range," Jessie said as they rode toward the area where the work was busiest. "And just at a guess, while we're riding down toward them we'd better be thinking about which is the best way to move in case trouble starts."

"You still figure we're going to have some

problems?" Wright asked as they drew closer to their objective.

"I hope we don't," Jessie replied. "But I'm sure we'll find out very soon. Now, the first thing we'll need to remember is that if we do have trouble, we stick together. We've already seen that we're pretty badly outnumbered."

"I don't imagine they'll give us any sort of a bad time, Miss Jessie," Wright put in. "And if they do start giving us trouble, I'll put my money on us being able to hold our own."

"Sure we can," Avery agreed. "And Ki's covering us from hiding."

"Then let's find out what happens when they see us," Jessie said. "This might not be the best time to risk a brush with the squatters, but there's no real way for us to avoid having one sooner or later."

Holding their horses to an easy walk, they started across the downslope. The trio had covered perhaps half the distance between them and the squatters across the downslope and were on level land before one of the group ahead noticed them.

Even at the distance that still had to be covered, Jessie and her two companions could see that the squatters were a tatterdemalion gathering. Most of the men were dressed like journeymen, in faded blue denim shirts and Levi's trousers. Jessie could glimpse a woman occasionally, but there were very few of them in the little crowd that was beginning to form in front of one of the big tents.

Jessie started to make a hit-or-miss count of the

33

group that was still some distance away, but the constant shifting of the little crowd and the arrival of newcomers defeated her efforts. She gave up after two or three tries, after she'd realized that in spite of the narrowing gap between her group and the squatters, both men and women wore clothing which was so much alike she'd been counting some of them twice.

When only a few yards separated Jessie and her companions from the growing crowd, she raised her voice and called to the nearest man, "Would you please tell me who's in charge of things here and point him out to me?"

Instead of replying with the information Jessie had requested, the man asked, "Strangers here, ain't you?" Then he answered his own question. "Me and these other folks has been together long enough for me to see right off that you ain't with our outfit."

"I might be a stranger to you," Jessie replied. "But my name is Jessica Starbuck, and I happen to own this land. It's part of my ranch, the Circle Star."

"Now, that can't be right," the man objected. A frown tinged with both perplexity and anger was forming on his face. "The land-office fellow back in Austin where we bought this spread give us a map, and we been following it every step of the way. It taken us a long time to get here, and if I know Pleas Barstow like I think I do, we sure ain't going to give it up on just your say-so!"

★
Chapter 4

For several moments Jessie did not reply to the man facing her. Then, with her voice held calmly level, she went on. "I've asked you to tell me the name of the man who's in charge of your group. From what you just said, I assume it's Pleas Barstow. Would you mind pointing him out to me?"

"It don't look like I'll have much pointing to do, lady," he replied. As he spoke he was raising his arm and gesturing toward the area behind Jessie and the men from the Circle Star. "That's Pleas right over yonder. He's the fellow in front of them others, the bareheaded one in a short-sleeve shirt, and I'd say he's heading thisaway."

Jessie as well as her companions twisted in their saddles to look in the direction the man was pointing. They saw a tall, husky horseman with a heavy jutting jaw leading four or five other riders. Unlike most of the group, the leader wore no hat, and even at a distance they could see a half-dozen raised lines of scar tissue, which extended from his eyebrows to his hairline. They could also see ragged raised scars on his bare forearms below the edges of his rolled-up sleeves.

Twisting in her saddle, Jessie dropped her voice to a half-whisper as she told Wright and Avery, "The best thing I can think of for us to do is to keep calm and stay in our saddles until that man we're waiting for gets here."

"You figure we're likely to have trouble?" Wright asked.

"Not any more trouble than we have now, I hope," she said.

Wright glanced again at the approaching man. "I don't mind telling you, Miss Jessie, I don't much like the looks of that Barstow fellow, to say nothing about the bunch he's got following him."

"Neither do I," Jessie agreed. "I can't say that I like the way Barstow looks, either, and I feel the same way that you do about those men with him."

"Well, you're likely to've run into as many of his kind as I have, Jessie," Wright commented. "We've both seen the drifters who've come to the Circle Star looking for work."

"Yes, there've been plenty of them," Jessie agreed.

Wright went on. "If he was to come to me asking for a job, I'd think twice before hiring him on, just like I've turned away quite a few men that I tagged right off as looking like troublemakers."

Jessie nodded. "I'd say that he's not going to be exactly friendly toward us when I break the news to him that his outfit's picked the wrong piece of land for setting up a new town."

Both Wright and Avery nodded also. By the time Jessie turned back to face the newcomers, Barstow and his little entourage had reached the fringe of the group that now surrounded Jessie and her two companions. Barstow motioned for the men with him to stop, and turned to say something to them before reining his horse to walk through the small crowd. Its members gave way as he pushed toward Jessie and the men from the Circle Star.

Barstow came to a halt a yard or so from Jessie and Wright and Avery. There was another flurry of subdued voices as the onlookers shifted around to close in on Barstow and the trio from the Circle Star.

For a moment Barstow said nothing, but flicked his eyes from Jessie to Wright and Avery before turning back to face Jessie. Then he asked, "You mind telling me who you are? And what kind of business brought you here?"

"My name is Starbuck," Jessie replied. "Jessica Starbuck. And I've heard the people crowding around us mention your name after we asked them who's in charge here. Unless I'm mistaken, it's Barstow."

"You called it right," Barstow agreed. "And I've heard about that big ranch called the Circle Star that you've got. Now go ahead and tell me what kind of business is so important that you've come here looking for me."

"Even though I'm sure I know the answers, there are two questions I need to ask you to begin with," Jessie replied.

"Fire away, then," Barstow invited.

"One is the same question you asked me a moment ago," Jessie told him. "I'd like to know who you are and what's brought you and your friends onto Circle Star range. The other is why somebody in your bunch here has been shooting at me and the men who're with me."

"Now, just you hold on for a minute, lady," Barstow said quickly. "We ain't on nobody's range. I can prove that to you in just about two minutes. And we ain't outlaws. We don't go around shooting at folks."

"That's very odd," Jessie said. "But the shots fired at us came from this direction."

Barstow hesitated for a moment before replying. "Well, now, maybe one of these folks with me did get a little bit trigger-happy. I wasn't paying much attention, but I sure didn't hear no guns go off."

"*We* certainly did," Jessie said quickly. "But that's in the past, and since nobody got hurt we'll push it aside for the moment. What's really important is finding out why you've come here on Circle Star range."

"Why, I'd say that all you need to do is look around and see what we've got in mind. We're settling here. We aim to start us a brand-new town."

Jessie nodded her head but said nothing. Barstow waited for her to speak, and when she did not reply, a puzzled frown wrinkled his face. When Barstow realized that Jessie had no intention to say anything, he went on.

"Now, if anybody in this outfit of mine has been shooting at you like you claim they have," he said, "it's because we been shot at a time or two on our way here and most of these fellows has got trigger-happy fingers."

"That's a very poor excuse," Jessie said. Her voice was firm as she went on. "I'm afraid you'll have to come up with a better reason."

Barstow did not respond immediately. Then he waved his hand toward the people that surrounded them. "I reckon I better tell you that there's a bunch more Galvanized Yankees than I can keep track of or than you can count on the fingers of both hands and all your toes thrown in. Or don't you know what Galvanized Yankee means?"

"Oh, I've heard the phrase before," Jessie replied. "Really mean veterans from General Grant's army, if I'm not mistaken."

"You called the turn," Barstow replied. "And maybe they're a mite trigger-happy, but don't try and tell us that we ain't got a right to defend ourselves."

"I'm not saying that at all," Jessie replied. "But my men don't shoot at strangers who've come on my range."

"Hold on now," Barstow bristled. "This here ain't your range, if it ever was. Me and these folks are claiming it as ours."

"I'm afraid that you won't be able to do that," Jessie told him. Her voice was level, neither threatening nor conciliatory, as she went on. "You're going to be disappointed in your plan to settle on this land, Mr. Barstow. You see, I own this section as well as the land on all four sides of it. They're part of my Circle Star ranch."

"The hell you say, lady!" Barstow snapped. "This here's open range, or was till me and these folks here bought it at the land office back in Austin. We're aiming to stay right where we are and build us a town."

A sudden babble of raised voices broke out at the fringe of the sizeable crowd that by this time had formed around Barstow and Jessie's small group. Jessie half turned as she looked for the source of the disturbance and saw Ki on horseback trying to open a path through the onlookers, one that would allow him to reach her and the two Circle Star hands. The packed bunch of spectators had grown larger and pressed even more closely together during the brief exchange between her and Barstow.

Jessie turned back to Barstow and said, "That man trying to get to us is from the Circle Star. Would you mind asking your people to let him through?"

Barstow hesitated for a moment, flicking his eyes from Ki to Jessie and Wright and Avery. Then he raised his voice and called, "Let the Chinaman get through! The lady wants him to come be here with her, and it won't hurt us a bit to oblige her!"

A flurry of movement started in the crowd congregated around Ki, but after a moment those nearest him were stepping aside to let him ride past. Ki reached the spot where Jessie and the other Circle Star men sat their horses. He did not dismount, but reined his horse toward Jessie.

Touching Sun's flank with a boot toe, Jessie twitched his reins and the big palomino began moving toward Ki. Barstow started to say something, but thought better of it and remained silent and motionless, watching the people in Jessie's path. They finally opened a narrow lane to let her through. Ki pulled up his mount to wait for Jessie, and when they came abreast she reined Sun in to bring him to a halt at Ki's side. Jessie raised her forefinger to place it across her lips. Ki nodded and leaned in his saddle until his head was close to hers.

"You don't need to waste time explaining," he

said, dropping his voice to a whisper. "I overheard enough to understand what's going on while I was trying to get through that bunch of people, so I know what's brought this crowd together."

"Then you know what our problem is," Jessie said, her soft voice matching Ki's whisper. "Suppose you come back with me while I try to break the logjam that fellow Barstow and I have gotten into. I don't want a fight to break out while there are only four of us against this crowd that's gathered."

Without waiting for Ki to reply, Jessie wheeled Sun again, and Ki followed her as the big palomino picked its way back to where Barstow was waiting. She noted that while she'd been gone a half-dozen men from the crowd had formed a close cluster around him.

Neither she nor Ki spoke, but they exchanged glances a time or two when they saw that other men who'd been at a distance when they first arrived were making their way to join the already large crowd which surrounded Barstow.

Jessie wasted no time. She began talking as soon as she was close enough to the squatters' leader for him to be able to hear her clearly.

"As I just told you, I'm afraid you're badly mistaken about this land we're on," she said. "This section of range belongs to me. I'm sure you've been here long enough to ride around a little bit, and you must've seen that it's fenced cattle-grazing land, not just open prairie."

"Oh, we did run into a fence or two," Barstow admitted. "But on the way from Austin to here we passed by lots of old busted-down fences with rusty bobwire. And there was plenty of posts without no bobwire where that land we seen used to be grazing range. Them places sure didn't look no different to me than this stretch of range we're on right now."

Jessie did not hurry to reply. After a moment she raised her arm and gestured with a sweeping move that took in the entire area and turned the heads of a number of the squatters to look momentarily around the disputed section of range.

Raising her voice in order to be heard by as many of the squatters as possible, Jessie said, "You've surely noticed that the barbwire fences that close off this piece of land aren't old and rusted out the way they would be if this section of my ranch wasn't being used for grazing. And it certainly isn't abandoned range, even if there aren't any steers on it at the moment."

"Now, steers or no steers sure don't mean nothing to us, lady," Barstow told her.

"It does to me," Jessie replied quickly. "Somehow you must've gotten your directions mixed up. I'm sorry to tell you this, but these people you've brought here will have to pack up and move on."

"Like hell we will!" Barstow snapped. "Even if I was to tell them to move someplace else, it ain't likely the Galvanized Yankees in my bunch would listen to me."

Jessie had hidden her growing annoyance during her long exchange with Barstow, but his immovable stance had irritated her from the beginning. There was an unaccustomed snappishness in the tone of her voice as she said, "I don't enjoy threatening anyone, Mr. Barstow, but if your people should refuse to move, I'll be forced to have my hands drive them off."

"And you think these folks'd pack up and go peaceful just on the say-so of your hired hands?" Barstow asked.

"Perhaps they wouldn't," Jessie replied. "In that case, I'd have no choice but to go to law and have them evicted."

"You try to pull a stunt like that, and you'll sure be sorry for it!" Barstow scowled. "Like I told you just a minute ago, we got a lot of Galvanized Yankees along with us. They're mean enough and tough enough to make anybody that'd try to keep us from building our town here wish they never had started any trouble."

"I'm not looking for trouble," Jessie assured him. "But remember that I've warned you. If your people carry out their threat of building on Circle Star range, I certainly don't intend to stand aside and do nothing."

"Maybe you'd better tell me just what you mean by that," Barstow suggested.

"I'll evict them, of course," Jessie replied. "The

law is on my side, as I'm sure you know." She turned to Ki and the pair of Circle Star hands who'd been beside her listening to the long drawn-out conversation she'd had with with Barstow. "We'd better go back to the main house now. I have an idea that Mr. Barstow will want to do some thinking about the talk we've had. And I'm just as sure that he'll want to be able to discuss what we've talked about without us being here."

None of her companions spoke, nor did Barstow. Jessie wheeled Sun around and toed him ahead. Ki followed her, as did Wright and Avery. Jessie paid little attention to the staring and murmuring crowd that had gathered around the spot where she'd had the exchange with Barstow.

Ki rode abreast of Jessie on one side, Wright and Avery on the other. Only after they'd gotten far enough away to be out of earshot of the small crowd that had gathered around Barstow did Jessie speak to her companions.

"That was an unpleasant few minutes," she said. "And I'm afraid things aren't going to get any better between us and those squatters."

"You believe they'll just stay where they are?" Ki asked.

"They're certainly not going to move out right now," Jessie replied. "If I'm any judge of character, that Barstow fellow won't even try to talk them into leaving, even if any of the squatters wanted to."

"I'll have to agree with you," Ki said. "I don't

think any more than you do that Barstow's going to do anything except sit tight."

"Then you figure we're going to have to fight them, Miss Jessie?" Avery asked.

"It's a little early to guess about that," Jessie replied. Her voice was thoughtful as she went on. "But I feel the same way that Ki does. We can't expect Barstow to give an inch, because if he does he's going to be in a lot of trouble with the squatters, and almost everything depends on what he does."

"I'm pretty sure the only things Barstow understands would be a fist to his jaw or a bullet," Wright put in. "And if it comes to a showdown, there's a lot more of them settlers than we've got hands on the Circle Star."

"Let's don't talk about a showdown, or even think about it," Ki suggested. "There's bound to be a peaceful way of settling this mess the squatters have brought us. The thing we have to do is find it."

★

Chapter 5

At last the long day was coming to a close. In the east the sky was already showing a tinge of deeper blue, and in the west only a small crescent of the setting sun was visible above the horizon. Wright and Jessie were standing at the Circle Star's horse corral.

"Remember, Ed," she said, "for the time being I'd like to keep our men away from that section of range the squatters have taken over. If it's possible, I want to avoid having any trouble with them."

"Keeping the hands away's not much of a job," the Circle Star foreman told her. "Most of them are out on the north range. They'll be bedding down in the line shacks for the better part of a week."

"Of course," Jessie said. "I'd almost forgotten that we just have a few hands left here after the Lazy S range got so overcrowded and we bought that new herd of steers from them."

"I'll see to it that the hands who're left here don't get crossways of that bunch of squatters," Wright said. "If you remember, I decided to split those new critters into two herds, so we wouldn't be in the same fix the Lazy S had gotten into. Then I had to spot the hands where they'd be needed the most."

"Then there shouldn't be any problems."

"None at all," he agreed. "At least until it comes time to handle the little day chores."

Ki had moved to Jessie's side while she and the foreman were talking. Before she could reply to Wright he said, "You and Ed go on making whatever plans you've been cooking up, Jessie. Unless you need me here, I'll see what Cookie's got in the way of food. Then I'll go on to the main house and make a start at fixing us some supper."

"Go ahead, Ki," Jessie said. As Ki started off, she turned back to Wright. "You used good judgment when you split the new steer herd, Ed. But let's get back for a minute to Barstow and his outfit. You and Avery have seen what they're like."

"We sure have," Wright replied. "And what I saw didn't make me like that bunch of squatters any better than I did before we got close to 'em."

Jessie nodded. "If either of you should get any ideas of what we ought to do about them, I'll be very glad to hear them. I'm certainly not interested in giving Barstow and his squatters an inch of Circle Star range. But I'll be ready to go along with anybody who has some ideas about getting him to move on without having to fight him."

"I sorta figured you'd say something like that," Wright said. "Now, I reckon I sized him up the same way you did. He's mean and he's smart all at the same time. I sure wouldn't trust him and his Galvanized Yankees for a minute."

"Oh, I wouldn't think of trusting him either," Jessie assured the foreman. "He's too puffed up with his own importance. And I've already tagged him as a man I'd think twice before trying to make any sort of deal with."

"There's one thing I did notice about what happened while we were talking to Barstow," Wright said. "When you and him got crossways, you didn't blow up or let on anything about him putting you out of sorts. It was easy to see that while you and him were having an argument you stayed calm, but he got real mad at you."

"Yes, he did," she agreed. "That's one reason why I cut our conversation short."

Nodding his head slowly, Wright said, "All of us know that when a man like Barstow loses his temper, he can be really dangerous, Jessie. Don't you think—"

Jessie broke in. "Don't worry, Ed. You know that Ki and I aren't likely to do anything foolish."

"I wasn't meaning to be—" Wright persisted.

Jessie raised her hand to silence him. "We've run across men like Barstow and his Galvanized Yankees before. And that brings up something else. To keep us from going off half-cocked, Ki and I need to sit down with you and make some kind of plan. Suppose you have breakfast with us in the morning, and we'll see what we can work out."

"I'll sure be there," Wright promised. "But if you'll excuse me now, I'm going to have to figure out where the hands will be working for the next couple of days. I know you're about ready to go up to the big house, so I'll take a final look around and you and Ki and me can do our talking early tomorrow."

Jessie nodded, and Wright started away. She watched him until his figure was lost in the gloom. Then she turned and began walking toward the main house. As Jessie had expected, Ki was waiting in the big room that was the heart of the Circle Star's headquarters. He'd placed a deep skillet on the broad hearth and was braising small fillets of beef in a dark sauce.

"What's happened in the cookshack?" Jessie asked. "I had an idea you'd just pick up our supper there like you do sometimes and bring it in here."

"Well, Cookie was just starting to get grub on

the table for Wright and the other hands," Ki replied. "So I decided it'd be better for me to keep out of his way."

"I know how Cookie is when he's busy." Jessie smiled. "And I suppose you're cooking our supper?"

"Of course," Ki answered. "I talked Cookie out of some fresh beef fillets he had on hand and I'm cooking them Japanese style. It's been quite some time since we've just sat down together for a quiet meal. Nobody's going to interrupt us, so we can talk during supper."

"I'm not sure that I want to do a great deal more talking tonight, Ki," Jessie said. "Even if we've got a lot to talk about. That Barstow fellow and his bunch gave me a very unpleasant surprise."

"Just as he did me," Ki confessed.

Jessie went on. "Besides, we've had a really busy day. Suppose we just eat supper and go to bed. We'll put off our talk until tomorrow morning."

"Whatever suits you best," Ki replied. "But it's going to take a little bit more time for this beef to cook. We can talk while we're waiting, if you've a mind to."

"We'll both be fresher in the morning, and those beef fillets smell very good indeed. And while I'm thinking of it, I've asked Ed to come and have breakfast with us in the morning, so in case we'll need some extra food we'll have to go and get it from Cookie."

"I'll remember to get up early and go to the

cookshack to pick up our breakfast victuals," Ki said. "But right now it looks like the meat's done. We'll both feel better after we've eaten."

Ki lifted the skillet off the coals and put it on the wide hearth. He served Jessie's plate, then his own, and both of them fell silent as they began eating. After they'd finished, Ki suggested, "Why don't you go on to bed, Jessie? I'll put these dishes aside and take them to the cookshack when I go across to get our breakfast in the morning."

"I'm sure that's the best thing I can do," Jessie agreed. "The idea of stretching out on a soft bed is very attractive right now. Good night, Ki."

Jessie suddenly sat up in her bed. She blinked a time or two, forcing the sleep from her eyes as she tried vainly to pierce the darkness of her curtained room. Then she realized that she had not been awakened by a noise, but by the unmistakable smell of smoke. This spur to her understanding brought her to her feet beside the bed, and two quick steps took her to the room's open window.

Pulling aside the drapes, Jessie leaned from the window and looked toward the back of the big house. Though she could see no flames, the full moon was obscured by a thin veil of smoke that shimmered in its refracted glow. The smoke was becoming almost invisible now as it trickled upward in the motionless air, and when Jessie looked up at the sky she could see that the shimmering white trails were rising from somewhere at the rear of the big house.

Now Jessie moved quickly. She sat up and jammed her bare feet into the boots that stood beside the bed, then grabbed the dressing gown that lay over the back of her bedside chair. Slipping her arms into the garment's sleeves, she pulled the gown around her and knotted its sash as she started for the door. She did not walk, but ran along the hallway to the door of Ki's bedroom at the opposite end of the corridor.

"Ki!" she called as she began rapping on the door with her knuckles. "Ki! Wake up! There's a fire somewhere close by, and I think its the house that's burning! Smoke's rising from behind it!"

Only a moment passed before Ki opened the door. Jessie's eyes had not yet shed all vestiges of sleep, and she was still blinking as Ki stepped into the hall. He was holding the folds of his singlet and trying to slip his hands into its sleeves.

"Are you sure the fire's behind the house?" he asked.

"I haven't gone to look," Jessie replied. "But a whiff of smoke came trickling in my bedroom window, and judging by the direction it was moving, I'm pretty sure that I'm right about it coming from somewhere at the back of the house."

"Then we'd better hurry and find out," Ki said. As he spoke he was still tugging at the singlet to get its armholes and shoulders in place. "Because now I can smell smoke in here."

Jessie was already starting down the hall. Ki hurried to follow her, and caught up with her as she reached the stairway. He asked, "You said you saw smoke coming from the back of the house, Jessie, but did you see any flames?"

"Maybe some little flickering glows, Ki. I never did see the fire itself, but it was burning, all right. I didn't want to waste any time going to look out of another window," Jessie answered as they started down the stairs.

"Then unless we see flames when we get outside, we'd better go around the house in different directions. Suppose you go out to the left and I'll go to the right."

"Good enough," Jessie replied. "That way we're sure to find it. But one of us has got to rouse Ed and have him send the hands that're still in the bunkhouse to help us."

"I'll do that and then come join you," Ki told her.

Ki was only a step behind Jessie when they reached the downstairs hall. He turned and said, "You can smell smoke here, all right, even if we don't know yet where the fire is."

"We know it's at the back of the house," Jessie told him.

"Of course," Ki agreed. "I'll go wake up Ed and tell him to rouse the hands while you go and see how bad the fire is. We ought to be able to see the blaze when we get outside."

Ki's prediction proved only partially correct. As

he and Jessie burst out of the front door, they could see only a few small spots of dim, dancing reddish glow coming from the back of the big house. Ki took one glance at the threatening flicker and started running toward the Circle Star foreman's house, which stood across the wide stretch of graveled road.

Jessie also began running, but in a direction opposite from the one Ki had taken. She skirted the side wall of the big mansion that her dead father had erected, and as she turned the corner and glanced along the rear wall Jessie gasped in dismay. There were flickering flames stretching along the base of the wall from the corner where she had stopped all the way to the far end of the big mansion.

Then as she looked more closely, Jessie could see that the flames were beginning to die away. She also saw that the small spurting blazes did not form a solid line, but were little dots of separate fires closely spaced.

After Jessie had gazed for a moment along what had been a seemingly unbroken line of red dancing flames, she breathed a sigh of mixed dismay and relief. Some of the little fires were still burning brightly, and a few of the red flickers were trying to crawl up the walls from the foundation of the big house. However, most of them were now beginning to diminish.

Only then did Jessie remember that when her father had planned and supervised the construction of the Circle Star's main house, he'd ordered that it be built with adobe brick walls instead of wooden planks. Suddenly the fire that had seemed so menacing only a short time past no longer held a threat. Jessie's tension had vanished by the time she saw Ki running toward her.

"You can relax, Ki!" she called. "The fire's almost dead now."

"You mean we aren't going to need the hands to help put it out?" Ki asked.

"I'm sure we won't," Jessie replied. "I suppose the best thing you can do is to hurry back and tell Wright we're sorry to've roused them, but the fire's gone out and they won't be needed."

"They aren't going to like it, but—"

"Tell them that even if they didn't get here there'll be some extra pay for their trouble. That ought to make them feel better."

"I'm sure it will," Ki agreed as he turned to go. "I'll only be gone a minute, Jessie."

Jessie gave up trying to examine the foundation line. Sure now that the flames would be defeated by the thick adobe walls, she hunkered down to wait for Ki to return. True to his promise, he was gone for only a minute or so. When he returned he was carrying a lighted lantern.

"If there's really a fire, we won't need this," Ki told Jessie. "But I thought we'd want to go along the foundation line. And after I'd stopped worrying about the fire, I remembered that when your father was building this house he realized that the adobe walls would need a good solid wooden foundation to keep the bottom courses of those adobe bricks dry."

"Then the foundation was what's been burning!" Jessie exclaimed.

"That's all," Ki said. "And that little flicker of fire hasn't done much damage because when the foundation was being put down your father held up the work on it for nearly a year, until he could get some special kind of a tropical wood. It's so solid that it just chars a little bit instead of burning."

"I suppose that's just what I might have expected of Father!" Jessie said. "Just the same, we'd better walk all the way around the house, Ki. There might be a place or two where the fire's not going out." As she was speaking, Jessie was turning her head away from Ki and looking along the bottom of the main house. "All but three or four of those little red splotches we saw when we first got here have died away."

"It's not likely that we'll see anything besides a few more of them," Ki said. "But we'll sleep a lot better if we do go along the side we haven't seen yet, and it won't take us any longer to go that way."

As he and Jessie started walking along the back wall of the big house, Ki went on. "I don't imagine that those men who tried to burn us out are still anywhere around here, or that they'd be easy to find, especially in the dark."

"At least we're sure that we know who set the fires, Ki," Jessie told him. "Or who had them set. I don't have any doubt at all about that. It was the squatters' boss, that Pleas Barstow fellow. He's the only one who could have sent that bunch here to try and burn us out."

"I don't have a bit more doubt about that than you do, Jessie," Ki said. "But how much chance do you think we'd have of proving it? He'd either lie or keep his mouth shut."

Jessie was silent for a moment. Then she replied, "We really don't have much choice, do we, Ki? If we ignore the fire they set tonight, it'll just give Barstow the idea that we're afraid to go back to that section he's trying to steal and face him down."

"We'd be going against a lot more people than we have hands, Jessie," Ki pointed out. "I didn't even try to count those squatters, to be sure of how badly we'd be outnumbered."

"My guess is that there are at least twenty," Jessie said. "At least that's what Avery told us. I'm quite sure we didn't see all of them when we were on that upper range. It's quite possible there are more. But regardless of how many we're up against, we have to get this mess settled down without losing any time."

"That goes without saying," Ki agreed.

★

Chapter 6

Ed Wright raised his hand to knock again on the door of the main house just as Ki opened it. After they'd exchanged good mornings Ki said, "I hope you didn't have any trouble getting back to sleep last night, Ed, after all the fuss-up about that false fire alarm."

"Why, I slept like a log. But I'll admit that I sure was tempted to come over here, even after you'd been back to let me know there wasn't any need to call out the hands. Did something happen that I missed?"

"Not a thing. As far as Jessie and I could tell, whoever set the fire—"

"Meaning the squatters, of course."

"Yes, it had to be some of those people Barstow's brought in," Ki agreed. "It couldn't've been anybody else. I'm sure they must've had everything planned out, because Jessie and I didn't hear any strange noises before the fires started."

"And not a shot was fired," Wright noted. "They certainly must've been careful, because none of us saw them or heard them."

"No shots and no noise, at least none that any of us heard," Ki observed. "Just to be safe, Jessie and I waited and watched until all the fires had flickered and died away. We didn't see or hear anybody moving."

By this time Ki and Wright were entering the dining room. Jessie and Wright exchanged good mornings. Then she gestured toward the table, which already held a platter of biscuits wrapped in a napkin to keep them warm. The table was set for three.

"Let's sit down and eat, Ed," she said. "We'll just forget about the unpleasant things that've happened and enjoy our breakfast. And I'm sure we'll agree to put aside problems and planning until after we've eaten."

"That'll suit me to a tee, Miss Jessie," Wright agreed.

"Then I'll go get the food and we can sit down and start," Ki suggested. "I don't know how Jessie and you feel, Ed, but my stomach's been telling me for quite a while that it's breakfast time."

"And so has mine," Jessie agreed. "Go ahead, Ki."

Soon after Jessie and Wright had seated themselves Ki returned, carrying three large platters. Each of them held a chicken breast covered with a white sauce. Ki placed the platters on the table and sat down in the vacant chair at one end of the table. Jessie gestured for them to begin, and they fell to.

None of the trio talked a great deal while they were eating the breakfast which Jessie and Ki had created from the generous choice of victuals from the airtights in the pantry. At last Wright pushed his plate away and turned to Jessie.

"You know, I don't mind admitting that I'd enjoy a breakfast like this every morning, Jessie," he said. "Not that I'm complaining about Cookie. His breakfasts are always good, even if they're pretty much the same, ham or bacon and hot biscuits or flapjacks and syrup. They don't run to the sort of victuals you've set out for us to enjoy."

"Don't give me too much credit." Jessie smiled. "And we certainly don't eat this fancy food every morning. Generally, Ki goes over to the cookshack and brings back just what you and the hands have, but this morning I suggested that he open some of the airtights that we get from back East."

"Well, it was sure a fine meal, and I thank you for inviting me to share it," Wright said. "But hadn't we better get down to brass tacks?"

"You're right, Ed," Jessie agreed. "And to start our brass-tacks talk, I've been trying to think of some peaceful way to get those squatters off

61

Circle Star range, and I know that Ki has, too."

Before Wright could reply, Ki spoke up. "We saw and heard enough yesterday to know what the situation is. As long as that Pleas Barstow is in command of the squatters, Jessie and I agree that it's going to take more than just asking Barstow to move on. All that he'd do would be to laugh at us."

"And we decided that we don't have enough hands to drive them off," Jessie said. "Barstow's got twenty, thirty people out there, and I won't ask our Circle Star men to fight against odds like that."

"They'd be with you all the way if you did ask them," Wright said. "Even if they did have to face Barstow's Galvanized Yankees. I heard enough of the hands talking at supper after we'd gotten back from our brush with the squatters to be sure of that."

"I can't ask our men to fight the settlers, Ed!" Jessie exclaimed. "When they hired on they expected to be ranch hands, not lawmen or soldiers. I'm sure that there are plenty of men who used to be soldiers in that bunch Barstow's got backing him up."

"I get your meaning, Jessie," Wright told her. "You don't think it's right for one bunch of soldiers to fight another bunch who might've fought side by side with them."

"Do you think it's right?" Jessie asked.

Wright did not reply for a moment. Then he

said, "Maybe it is and maybe it's not. But it wouldn't be the first time it's happened. Those war veterans that call themselves Galvanized Yankees are about as tough as boot soles. They won't care who they fight, and I don't look for our fellows to be any different."

"There's bound to be a way to solve this problem, even if we don't see it right now," Ki said.

"I'm afraid it's not going to be an easy one to solve, Ki," Jessie told him. "We certainly can't treat the squatters like they're a bunch of outlaws, even if that Barstow fellow acts like he might have been one at some time or other."

"But supposing we can't . . ." Wright began. He broke off as a thunking of hoofbeats reached their ears from outside the house. "Jessie, the way that horse is being pushed so hard has got to mean that somebody's real anxious to get here. Likely it's one of the hands looking for me, so I'd better go see what it's all about."

Wright had been getting to his feet as he spoke. He started for the door, and Jessie and Ki left the table to follow him. They reached the front door in time to see a rider wheeling his lathered horse across the expanse of bare ground in front of the main house and reining it toward the little cluster of cabins that were scattered beyond the bunkhouse.

"That's Fred Ellis, the new hand I hired on month before last!" Wright exclaimed. "And he's likely got some kind of trouble to unload on me, looking for me." Raising his voice, he shouted, "Ellis! If you're looking for me, swing back around this way!"

When he heard Wright's voice the rider reined up his mount and then headed it to where Jessie and Ki and Wright were standing. He started tugging his reins as he neared the house, and came to a halt in front of the little group that was waiting on the veranda. Wright stepped toward the man astride the lathered horse.

"What's wrong, Fred?" he asked. "It has to be important since you're in a pretty big hurry to find me."

"Them damn rustlers have been busy again," Ellis said. "The fence-cutting bunch that we've had hit us before."

"Damn it, man!" Wright exclaimed. "That's just what you were put there to stop!"

"But I was on the other side of the range!" Ellis protested. "I bedded down on my saddle blanket last night because I'd stayed too long on the other side of that big hump that runs across the prairie. I got caught in the dark there and my nag was starting to limp."

"Well, that'd make a difference, I guess," Wright said. "Now what's all this about the fence-cutters?"

"I'd finished with the back range yesterday," Ellis began. "So I figured to ride the fence line along the front range today. I started on the north range about daybreak, right after I got up and had a bite of breakfast."

"Just skip over what we don't have to know about and tell us what we don't know yet," Jessie suggested.

"Sure, Miss Jessie," Ellis said. "I had to follow the fence line for a spell to get to the herd. That's when I saw the first signs somebody'd been there when I wasn't around. Like I said, I could tell they'd been there even before I got close to the herd. The critters was all scattered out and spooked, so the cattle-snatchers couldn't've been gone very long."

"Did you tally?" Wright asked.

Ellis shook his head. "I didn't see how I could put off starting here to find you. I could tell there was something wrong just by looking at the herd. Then I seen where the bobwire was cut out and I had a pretty good idea about what had happened, but I figured it'd be better for me to hustle back here and tell you about the rustlers than put in a lot of time tallying."

"I think you did just the right thing," Jessie told him. "I'm sure you spliced up the place where the rustlers had cut the range fence?"

"Oh, sure, Miss Jessie," Ellis replied. "I could see how it was with the critters all scattered and spooked. Right then I knew I had to fix up whatever was needed to keep the rest of the steers from getting out, so I done the best I could.

"I also seen something else. There was

wagon-wheel ruts all along the fence for a pretty good stretch from where I was. Then I looked around and seen couple of buzzards on the ground a little ways off, and when I seen they was eating steer guts I didn't take time to do anything but come back here."

"I guess that's all we need," Wright told Jessie and Ki. He turned back to Ellis and asked, "How come you didn't bring your rifle?"

"Like I said a minute ago, I didn't think about much of anything except getting here to tell you-all about what I'd run into," Ellis replied. "But I'll do all right with my Colt."

"Let's forget about everything but the rustlers, then," Jessie said.

"We'd better get moving right away," Ki said quickly.

"Ki's right," Jessie said. Turning to Wright, she went on. "Ed, we want those cattle thieves and we know they had a wagon. It ought to leave an easy trail to follow, especially if it has a big load on it."

"Oh, sure," the foreman agreed.

"Don't you suppose that if we start following the fence line from where we are here, slanting off it when we're maybe a half mile from where the fence was cut, we could track that wagon's wheel ruts?" she asked.

"A set of wagon ruts sure ought not be hard to follow," Wright agreed. "And a wagon with a steer carcass or two is bound to leave a clear trail."

"And the cattle thieves will drive those steer carcasses all the way back to that section where Barstow's bunch is fixing to build their town," Jessie said.

"That's probably where they're going," Ki agreed.

"And they'd be likely to stop somewhere along the way instead of carrying a wagonload of meat to where the squatters are," Jessie said. "I imagine they'd take time to skin and quarter out the steers they stole. They certainly wouldn't try to do much more. Then they'd load the meat on their wagon and go back to where they're getting ready to build their town. But we've got to catch up with them, even if they wouldn't be carrying anything except dead meat."

"It wouldn't take them a lot of time to do that kind of job, either," Wright put in.

"You're right about that, Ed. And we'd have no way to prove that the meat came from one of my herds," Jessie agreed. A frown was forming on her face. "But I certainly don't intend to let Barstow's people feed on Circle Star steers any more than I intend to let them stay where they are now, on Circle Star range."

"If they've got a load of beef on a wagon, they won't be making very good time," Ki pointed out. "And their load's heavy. Their wheel tracks will be fresh and deep. We ought not have any trouble following them."

"You've convinced me, Ki," Jessie said. She

turned to Wright. "Let's pick up their trail and go after them, Ed."

"You don't think they've got too much of a lead on us? Enough that it's going to make it hard for us to catch up?" Wright asked her.

"It's not likely they have," Jessie told him. "Ki was right. They'll be moving slowly on that long upslope that's in their way."

"And once we get past it, we'll be moving a lot faster than a loaded wagon can," Wright agreed.

"Even if we lose their trail we can ride zigzags to pick it up," Ki reminded them. "And since all these confused footprints and hoofprints don't give us much of a clue about how many of them there are, we'd better take Ellis with us."

"And I'm real ready to go, too!" Ellis exclaimed.

Jessie did not speak for a moment, then she said thoughtfully, "I suppose you're right, Ki. We can leave his part of the range without a rider for a day or so."

"Then you and Ki ride ahead, Jessie," Wright suggested. "I know you've both got good trail eyes."

After a moment of confused shifting and turning, the little group of pursuers set out, angling to save time in crossing the the fresh wagon-wheel ruts. The ground was soft, and where the grass did not grow too thickly, the laden wagon they were following had left deep grooves in it, new ruts that were easy to spot from horseback.

Occasionally they came to barren stretches of

baked soil where the wheel ruts vanished, but these were so few and so small that they did little to slow down the pursuing riders. A few minutes circling was the only thing required to find the trail again.

They reached the crest of the long upslope, and a long stretch of level grassland became visible in front of them. After they'd covered what seemed to be a very long distance, Jessie suddenly stood up in her stirrups and pointed ahead.

"Look! There's the wagon!" she exclaimed. "And it's not too far ahead! We've finally caught up with them!"

★

Chapter 7

When Jessie's companions heard her call, they were quick to follow her example. They stood up in their stirrups and began peering ahead at the wagon. There was still too great a distance between them and the slow-moving vehicle ahead to make out any of its details. Jessie toed her mount to a faster gait and the others followed her example.

Soon the downslope which the wagon had been crossing gave way to a short expanse of level ground. Beyond it the land began a long gentle rise. No one in Jessie's little party spoke, their full attention fixed on the wagon. Several minutes more ticked off before its high rear wheels became clearly visible. Then the blocky end of its tailgate, as well as the outlined figures of its driver and

71

the man on the seat beside him, could be seen clearly.

"As nearly as I can make out there are only two men in that wagon ahead," Jessie called to Ki. He was the rider nearest her. Beyond him Wright and Ellis were riding abreast.

"Look a bit closer, Jessie, and you'll see three," Ki told her. "One of them's not easy to catch sight of. He's lying down on the tarp they used to cover up their load of stolen beef in the wagon bed."

"Yes, I see him stretched out there now," Jessie agreed. "And for the last half mile I've been thinking about pulling my rifle out of my saddle scabbard and taking a shot or two at them."

"Wouldn't it be better to wait until we're closer?" Ki asked. "So far they haven't caught on that we're following them, and all that's ahead for the next few miles is open range. On this rise we'll be moving a lot faster than they will."

"Don't worry, I'll be patient, Ki," Jessie replied. "But let's try to catch up with them now, because if I remember the way the land lays, there's a downgrade on the other side of this rise, and that wagon will be able to make almost as good time going across it as we can on our horses."

"That's something I can't argue about," Ki told her. "And you're right about the lay of the land."

Jessie spurred to a faster pace. The others followed her example and little by little, the distance between them and the wagon diminished. It was easier now for them to determine just how slowly it was moving, and they could tell by its leisurely progress and the straining of the plodding horse pulling it that the wagon bed held a heavy load. They were close enough now to see its three occupants quite clearly, but were still too far away to distinguish anything but their backs.

Two men occupied the wagon seat; the third was now hunkered down in the wagon bed just behind his companions. While their voices were lost in the distance, it was apparent from their frequent gestures that the topic of their discussion was not a totally friendly one. As their exchanges became more and more heated, one of the trio raised his arms while shaking his head vigorously and bending forward, stretching his neck until his nose was almost brushing the nose of the man with whom he was arguing. At times their discussions were prolonged and lasted for several minutes.

"I can't understand why they haven't spotted us yet," Ki said thoughtfully. He kept his eyes fixed on the wagon and its riders, whose discussions were still going on. "But it's just a question of time now before they will."

"You're right, Ki," Jessie agreed. "Let's hope they keep so busy talking that they won't look back and see us." She turned to Wright. "Perhaps we'd better speed up and catch up with them. If we're lucky they won't notice us until we're a bit closer."

"Then hadn't we better start covering them with our rifles?" Ellis asked. "Sometime inside of the next few minutes they're bound to see us. And when they do they're surely going to begin trying to pick us off."

"I'm not sure how much good they can do," Jessie said. "Or how much harm, if you want to put it the right way."

"It'll be easy enough for us to ride zigzags if they start shooting," Wright suggested. "There's no creeks or sumps anyplace on this part of the range. I know it pretty well, because I've had to let off a shot or two at lobos while I was riding this part of the prairie."

"It won't take them long to find out that the range is a bit too long and the ground is too bumpy for good shooting out of a wagon," Ki put in. Wright nodded. "But it certainly won't do any harm to be ready."

"I'd be the last to disagree with you," Jessie told Wright. She was sliding her rifle from its saddle scabbard as she spoke. Ellis followed her example, pulling out his own rifle he balanced the weapon across the pommel of his saddle. Ki slid open the narrow slit of leather that held the overlap of the leather case on his forearm in which he carried his *shuriken*.

"I'd say we're about as ready as it's possible for us to be," Jessie said calmly. "If those men in the wagon ever get through arguing and look back, they're going to get some unpleasant surprises.

And I'd take it as a favor if you men will let me have the first shot."

Jessie's words might have been a prophecy. As though her remark had been a cue, one of the men in the wagon seat turned to say something or reply to a remark that had been made by the man in the wagon bed. For a moment it was apparent to the trailing riders that the man who'd discovered them was half stunned by the shock of learning that the wagon was being followed.

He turned to the other man in the wagon seat, his moving hands pointing and gesticulating, but this time he was pointing toward Jessie and her small force. At the same time the man in the wagon bed scrambled to his feet, followed by both men in the wagon seat.

One of the men arising from the wagon seat held a rifle, while the man beside him fought the now-tangled reins. Jessie had been holding her Winchester on a slant across her chest. Shouldering it quickly, she picked the man holding the rifle as her target and fanned the weapon until its sights were squarely on him.

In the wagon all three of the men were now turning to face their pursuers when Jessie's shot cracked. The man was just raising his own rifle when her slug went home. Before the reverberations from the Winchester stopped rippling the air he began sagging slowly to the wagon bed.

His body was still folding downward when

Wright loosed a shot. Its bark sounded just as the wagon driver was bringing up his rifle. The slug from Wright's weapon struck the stock of the man's rifle. The bullet's impact tore the weapon from his hands and sent it spinning to the bottom of the wagon bed. As he was bending to pick it up, one of the wagon wheels jounced over a grass-covered ridge and sent him tumbling to the wagon bed.

Jessie had levered a second round into the chamber of her rifle during the few moments that followed the first shot. By this time the man in the wagon bed was clawing frantically for his holstered revolver.

Jessie's second bullet and Ki's *shuriken* hit him at almost the same instant. The speeding slug from her Winchester and Ki's razor-sharp blade biting into his face did their deadly task. Their target's arms went up convulsively as he struggled for balance during the few moments of life that remained to him. Then he sagged to the wagon bed and lay still.

"That's enough, you folks!" the surviving man called in a hoarsely weak voice. "We're whupped! I give in!"

"Then get your arms up over your head!" Wright called.

"And keep them there!" Jessie added quickly. "Don't make a move while we're riding to you, or you'll be as dead as those men with you are!"

"You got nothing to worry about, lady!" the

survivor assured her. "I got sense enough to know when I'm licked!"

As Jessie and Ki rode abreast toward the wagon, neither they nor their companions took their eyes off the man who'd survived their attack. The wide stretch of land seemed endless, but they neither dawdled nor hurried, and Jessie was careful to keep the wagon's occupant covered.

It was a bloody scene that greeted the Circle Star riders when they reached the wagon and reined in beside it. The wagoner was still holding his hands above his head, the motionless bodies of the two dead men who'd started the fracas lying in crumpled heaps over the canvas that covered the wagon's load.

Almost before they'd dropped the reins of their horses, the survivor of the fracas broke the silence that had settled over the bloody scene after the shooting stopped.

"I been holding up my hands so long that my arms is sure hurting," he said. "Can't I let 'em down now?"

Ki and Ed Wright looked questioningly at Jessie. She'd reined in a short distance from the wagon and was looking at the two bodies sprawled out on the blood-smeared canvas. She did not reply to the driver's request nor to the questioning glances of Ki and Ed Wright. She took her time surveying the wagon bed, then asked the wagoner, "That pistol on the seat, is it yours?"

"Yes, ma'am, it is," he answered.

"Then pick it up by the end of the barrel and toss it to the ground," Jessie said. She turned to Ki. "Ki, after you've searched this fellow to make sure he doesn't have any more weapons, tie his hands behind him."

"Right away, Jessie," he replied as he dismounted and started for the wagon. "But one of you'd better keep an eye on him until I find some rope."

"There's some short pieces under the wagon seat," the man volunteered. "It ain't nothing fancy, just butcher's twine, but it holds a knot real good."

Wright's jaw dropped in surprise when he heard the reply, but he said nothing. He and Jessie watched in silence while Ki rummaged under the wagon seat and brought out a small coil of rope entangled with a canvas bag. Gesturing to their prisoner to lean forward in his seat, he untangled the rope.

For a minute Ki held the bag in his hand, debating whether to toss it to the ground, for by its weight and bulk it held only gunpowder. At last he dropped the bag to the wagon bed and got busy binding the man's wrists together. It took him only a moment to bring up the bight of the rope, pass it around the captive's elbows, and pull them close to his ribs.

When he was sure that his knots were secure Ki stepped aside and turned to Jessie. "You ought not have any trouble guessing what that wagon's loaded with, Jessie."

"I'm sure I won't," she agreed. "A steer carcass, isn't it?"

"Butchered, skinned, and quartered," Ki replied. "Just as we were sure that's what it would be. But there's no sign of the hide with the Circle Star brand on it. The only thing in the wagon besides the carcass is a bag of gunpowder."

"So the fellow we've got tied up in the wagon is a cattle thief," Jessie said. Then she raised her voice to make sure their captive would hear her. "Shall we just hang him here, or take him back to the Circle Star and find out who he's in cahoots with?"

"That's for you to decide," Ki replied. "One thing's sure, he won't be making any more trouble for us."

Jessie did not speak at once. Her eyes were flicking along the bed of the wagon. The man who'd fallen to one of their shots lay in a cramped, curled-up heap, halfway under the seat. The other was sprawled in an ungainly stretch, lying across the tarpaulin. One of his legs was still lodged on the back of the wagon's seat, his body extending along the tarpaulin that hid the butchered steer. His rifle was lying across his chest.

When Jessie had finished her brief scrutiny she turned back to the man Ki had tied up and said, "Now that we're sure you won't give us any more trouble, you can answer my questions."

"Supposing that I don't," he said, challenge

79

creeping into the tone of his voice. "What do you aim to do then?"

"Why, that should be easy for you to guess," Jessie replied. As she was speaking, Jessie waved her hand toward the bodies of the wagoner's companions.

"Now, hold on a minute!" the man protested. "You ain't meaning to say that you'd shoot me in cold blood!"

"You just saw what happened to those men who were with you," Jessie replied. "And if there was a tree close by that we could string you up on, we might save ourselves a bullet." Her voice was iceberg-cold as she went on. "But since there isn't . . ." She stopped speaking and lifted her rifle by its stock.

For a moment the wagoner made no response. Then he said, "I reckon I got sense enough to know when I'm whupped. Go on and ask me whatever you want to."

"What I want you to tell us first is your name, then the name of the man who sent you here," Jessie said. "Even if I'm sure that I know what his name is as well as I do, I want you to speak it in front of these witnesses."

Hesitating for only a moment, their captive replied slowly, his brows wrinkled into a puzzled frown. "Well, I don't reckon you'd have much trouble finding my name out. All you'd need to is ask anybody up at the new settlement. It's Cletus Berle."

Jessie nodded. "And the name of the man who sent you here?"

"Hold up, lady. I can't see what all this ruckus is about. All you'd need to do is ask anybody up at the settlement, and I know you been there because I seen you yesterday. But just to satisfy you, it was Pleas Barstow that sent me. And you're sure to know he's the same one that's got the say with them folks up on that section that you claim belongs to you."

"Of course I know Pleas Barstow's name," Jessie replied. "And I certainly know quite well that he's bossing a lot more people than just you. But I told you to say his name so these men with me can testify in court that they heard you call it."

"Now, I don't see how you aim to take nobody to court," Ellis said, looking puzzled. "Pleas swore to us that if we was to get caught he could get us off."

"Then he lied to you," Jessie said. "Just like he did about the land you're squatting on."

"Pleas says you ain't got the chance of a snowball in hell of making us move off that land," Berle stated. "But I don't see that you'd be fool enough to want getting crossways of him, because *I* sure don't."

"You've already gotten mixed up in it, just like the rest of the people following him have," Jessie replied. "But I've gotten all I need, now that every one of us has just heard you admit that Barstow's your boss."

81

"And we're all ready to stand up in court and testify to what was said," Ki added. "There's no way at all for you to get off scot-free."

Jessie nodded, then returned her attention to their captive. "I suppose you understand that now we've heard you confess to being cattle rustlers. And we've also caught you with stolen cattle in your wagon."

"It ain't my wagon!" Berle protested. "And I can prove that!"

"That doesn't make any difference," Jessie said calmly. "But there may be a way for you to save your worthless skin. Barstow is going to face cattle-rustling charges just as you are, since he's the one who ordered you to—"

"Wait a minute, lady!" Berle broke in. "If I was—"

Ignoring him, Jessie plunged ahead. "Before this is finished, you can go to prison with Barstow. I just wonder what he'd do to you if you're both in the same cell."

For a moment the captive rustler stared at her, his jaw dropping. He gulped, and tried to speak, but no words came out.

Jessie broke the silence. "I can see that you know what would happen if you and Barstow shared a prison cell."

"Now, you listen, lady," Berle began.

"Suppose *you* listen," Jessie said. "I can arrange for you to be in the same cell with Barstow. Do you think he'd let you stay alive to testify against him?"

"Wait up, now!" Berle told her, raising his voice to override hers. "You're trying to spook me! Barstow wouldn't be all that mean! We'd be in the same mess!"

"You know better than that," Jessie went on calmly. "Once Barstow learns the whole story— and I'll see that he does—how long do you think it'd take for him to get rid of you?"

"Now listen, lady, you tricked me into saying what I just did," Berle told her. "And if you think I'm . . ."

"Going to the gallows?" Jessie finished. "Of course you are. But not if you're in the same jail with Barstow, take my word for that."

"What're you getting at?" Berle asked.

"Just think about it for a minute," Jessie suggested. "If we let you stay alive and take you to the squatters' camp, he'll be wanting to get rid of anybody who can testify against him."

"Testify to what?"

"That he sent you out to steal cattle while you were helping him in a scheme to rob the United States Government and a lot of innocent settlers. Don't make the mistake of thinking that he's going to get away with this plan he's trying to pull off."

"But why would he be after me?"

"I'm sure you know the law says you're both rustlers. Both of you would be guilty and Barstow knows it. Of course, he could kill you himself to keep you from testifying against him, but it's more likely he'd get one of his Galvanized Yankees to do the job." Turning away from Berle, Jessie raised her voice and called, "Let's start moving again! We've still got a lot of business to take care of before it gets dark!"

★

Chapter 8

"Even if we're sure that Barstow's not letting any grass grow under his feet, we need to keep track of what he's doing," Jessie remarked, speaking to Ki over her shoulder.

Lifting her rifle, she stood up in her stirrups, trying to get a look beyond the spot where they'd stopped. When she found that she was not tall enough to see anything over the rim of the rise, she nudged Sun with her boot toe and reined him to the wagon.

Ki had brought the wagon to a halt before it reached the point beyond the rise where it would be visible to the squatters. A few paces away Wright and Ellis were dismounting. They'd discovered that if they stayed in their saddles they'd risk being seen above the top rim of

85

the upslope. They stopped long enough beside the horses to pull their rifles from their saddle scabbards before starting toward Jessie and Ki.

Jessie was checking the loads in her rifle while Berle, still restrained by his bonds, was twisting and straining to lift himself in order to see over the wagon's high sides. Jessie noted his efforts and stepped up to the wagon.

"Don't make any mistakes now, like trying to break free," she warned him. "Just remember, you're lucky to be alive."

Her words stopped their captive's squirming. Berle stretched out as best he could as he replied, "Why, I ain't a bit worried, lady. I know where we're at, and it ain't going to be too long before one of our bunch runs across this wagon."

"You think they'll come and set you free?" Jessie asked.

"Maybe so and maybe not, but they'll be bound to wonder what it's doing here. If they get curious enough they'll ask somebody about it. Then whoever they've asked is likely to come to find out why the wagon's stopped here where it is instead of pulling into the middle of our camp like it generally does."

Jessie did not bother to reply to their captive's hopeful remark. She had been the one to make a snap decision that it would be profitable for them to pull behind the rise and make a quick preliminary investigation before going into the squatters' camp. Ki's choice of a stopping place was the narrow strip of flatland hidden from the terrain beyond the long, low-rising hump which now sheltered them from being seen by the squatters.

Wright and Ellis now came to join Jessie and Ki.

"Jessie, are you figuring to go right to the middle of the place where Barstow's got the squatters scattered all over?" Wright asked.

"Right now I don't have any plan except to find out what they're doing," Jessie replied. "Surely the idea of being so close to them doesn't bother you, Ed?"

"Now, you know that's not it, Jessie," the Circle Star foreman replied. "But I know how you feel about us taking chances unless we've got to, and I'd say Barstow sent you a signal without wasting any too much time."

"You're talking about the fire he had his Galvanized Yankees set to burn down the main house?" Jessie asked. Wright nodded, and she went on. "I'm sure that all of us understand what Barstow's trying to do."

"Of course," Ki broke in. "He might just as well have told us in plain English that he's downright set on getting the people with him to hurry and get started settling in."

"And right now him and his Galvanized Yankees are holding the edge on us while we're still wondering how we can stop the squatters from taking Circle Star land without us getting into a shooting match," Wright added.

"Of course," Jessie agreed. "But I've already decided that unless we can get Barstow's outfit to move on peacefully to some other place where they can settle in, I intend to call all our hands in off the range and give him a real shooting match."

"Now, Jessie, Barstow's no fool," Wright said. "He knows we're outnumbered, and my guess is that he'll stand pat if he's not sure we've got enough men to force him to leave."

"Fighting the squatters isn't my idea of the best solution either, Jessie," Ki put in quickly. "But do you think it would do any good if you told him you'd buy him off?"

"No, I don't, Ki," Jessie replied. "No matter how much I offered Barstow, I'd just be wasting my breath. And nothing's going to change the fact that we're outnumbered even with all our hands available. But let's don't waste time talking. Let's get up on that rise and see what the squatters are doing."

"Don't you think one of us ought to stay behind to make sure that Berle fellow doesn't try to get away?" Ellis asked.

Jessie shook her head as she said, "No. He can't get those bonds loose, so just let your reins drop. You're new to ranch horses, and I don't suppose anybody's told you yet that every horse on my range is trained to stand when it's saddled and doesn't have a rider on its back. There's got to be somebody in the saddle, or leading it."

Advancing slowly and cautiously, keeping well apart, they started on foot up the low rise. All of them dropped their jaws in a mixture of surprise and anger at their first glimpse of the busy scene that stretched in front of them. In the center of the area claimed by the squatters, the big tent that they'd seen spread on the ground at the time of their earlier visit was now in the process of being erected. Its huge span of canvas was completely stretched on the ground, and a dozen or more men were busy carrying long thick tent poles to the edges of the substantial area it covered.

When Jessie and her group flicked their eyes away from the tent and surveyed the bottom of the oval of grass-covered ground in their first sweeping look, it seemed that men were busy at work in every spot that caught their eyes. Dotting the ground away from the wide span of canvas were a dozen or more smaller tents. Here and there, following no plan that they could make out, were makeshift lean-tos designed to protect blankets or quilts.

There were a number of places where only rumpled blankets and the ashes of small dead cooking fires marked areas which had been claimed by one of the squatters.

In a half-dozen widely separated spots distant from the tents and wagons and the improvised corrals men were shoveling to level small areas.

Some were tossing the clods of earth into wheelbarrows, while others were dumping the soil onto squares of canvas. At such places there was always a horse or a mule waiting to drag away the canvas squares that had been heaped with loose soil.

"I don't have any use for that Barstow fellow," Ki said after they'd watched the busy activity for several moments. "But he's sure put those squatters to work without wasting any time."

"Much too fast to please me," Jessie said. "All we can do is guess about the places that are going to wind up as houses and which will be stores."

"We can see something else, Jessie," Wright told her. His voice was sober. "I've watched enough new towns go up to know that at the rate these people are working, once they get in a load of lumber it's not going to take them very long to hammer up a pretty good sized bunch of real buildings."

"That's the same thing bothering me right now," Jessie said. Anger began tinging her voice. "They're certainly ruining a lot of the Circle Star's good cattle-grazing range. We've got to stop this before they get too far along!"

"Well, we haven't had enough free time to've even thought that the squatters would be getting busy so quickly," Ki replied. His usually expressionless face was puckered into an unaccustomed frown as he turned to Jessie. "But isn't there a legal way for you to stop this squatter town from being built on land that belongs to you?"

"Oh, I'm sure there is," she said. "But it would take us several days just to get to my lawyers, and that would only be the start."

"It might save a lot of shooting, though," Wright said thoughtfully. "Not that I'm trying to back away from a fight."

"All of us know that, Ed," Jessie agreed. "But I'm shy of lawyers myself. By the time they'd finished looking for the proper law books and going through them to find out just exactly how the papers have to be worded, and then getting the pleas and petitions ready and filing them in the nearest court, the squatters would have their town built and be living in it."

"Yes, I remember how much time and trouble your father once had to go through just to get together all the papers he needed when his lawyers were getting a suit ready to file," Ki told her. "As I recall, he waited three or four months before his case went to court."

"Which should give us an even sharper spur to getting the squatters off Circle Star range," Jessie said. "But we won't get anywhere by dillydallying."

"If you mean that this isn't exactly the best place we could be in, I don't think any of us would argue about that," Ki reminded her. "And we've seen everything that's important. I'd say we ought to go back to where we left the horses."

Jessie did not speak for a moment, then she said, "There's no use in us having spent all this time for nothing, Ki. Let's just hold on here a minute while we make some kind of plan."

"I'm sure you're not thinking about trying to attack that bunch of people," Ki replied. "But just what kind of plan do you have in mind?"

"I've been thinking these past few minutes about you and me going into that squatters' nest and trying to convince Barstow that he's making a mistake by trying to build his town here."

"Do you really think we'd have even a small chance of doing that?" Ki asked. "Because I don't."

"Oh, neither do I," Jessie agreed. "And I know that what I just said was more wishful than practical. The squatters have already made up their minds to stay, and I'm sure they'd balk."

"If we threaten them they're bound to start fighting like fury to defend what they call their rights," Ki cautioned her. "It'd take more sticks of dynamite than we've got in the Circle Star's powder house to get them to move an inch."

"I'm certainly not going to blow up any part of the Circle Star, Ki," Jessie assured him. "But neither am I going to let a man like that Pleas Barstow steal an inch of my range."

"Speaking of the devil," Wright said, "isn't that Barstow over at the corner of that big tent they've got spread out?"

"It's him all right," Jessie said after she'd

glanced in the direction Ki pointed. "And from the way he's acting I'd guess that they're getting ready to raise the tent."

They fell silent for a moment, all of them watching the area which had suddenly become a beehive of activity as other squatters joined the small throng that had been forming around Barstow. He was in the center of the group, which now numbered fifteen or twenty, pointing to one man or another and then indicating with a gesture a section of the huge spread of canvas.

"They're getting ready to raise the tent, all right," Jessie said. "And if I had any way of stopping them, I'd certainly use it. I'd like to touch a few matches to it and watch it go up in flames!"

"I'm afraid it's too big a job to set it afire with nothing but matches, Jessie," Ki said. He stopped, Jessie's words jogging his memory. Then he went on. "Gunpowder's what we'd need, and there's a bag of it in the wagon, enough to set fire to that big tent a dozen times over. The only trouble is that we don't have a way to use it."

Jessie thought for a moment. Then she said, "Maybe we do have a way, Ki. That wagon has a canvas cover spread over the steer carcass with a lot of rope coiled up on it."

"I can see you're beginning to get an idea, Jessie," Ki said. "Go ahead and tell us what it is."

"If all of us work fast we can put together, oh,

93

maybe a dozen or more makeshift firebombs. All of them might not explode, but they sure will let off enough hot sparks to set almost anything afire. And that includes the big tent they're getting ready to raise."

Ki nodded. "It sounds like we'll need more time than we've got, but it's the only way I can see to make trouble for the squatters."

"Then let's give it a try!" Jessie exclaimed. "It's going to take them a while to get that tent properly spread out. I don't think they can be ready to start raising it in less than an hour or so. We'll just have to work fast!"

As Jessie finished speaking she was already heading toward the wagon. Ki and the others caught up with her as she was leaning over the wagon bed. Ki vaulted into the wagon bed and began dragging the bound Berle toward the tailgate.

"You mind telling me what in hell you're doing?" Berle asked. "You ain't going to toss me out and leave me to lay on the ground for somebody to—"

Ki broke in. "Never mind what's going to happen to you. Just answer my questions. I know you've got a bag of powder tucked away in here, and I'd imagine you've got some fuse cord, too. Is it under the wagon seat?"

Berle hesitated for only a moment before saying, "Looks to me like you won't be needing any help finding it, seeing as how you already know so much. I can't figure out any way I can stop you from helping yourself."

Jessie had begun probing under the seat. Now she called to Ki, "I've found the fuse cord."

Ki turned away from Berle and located the bag of powder in the wagon bed. "I'll get this back to the tailgate where we'll be working," he told Jessie. "And I'll check Berle's bonds to see that he won't break free and bother us."

Ki needed only a few minutes to move the powder and the fuse cord to the wagon's tailgate. He dropped the gate before lowering himself to the ground. He pulled the edge of the canvas that had covered the wagon's load to the back edge of the wagon bed and began cutting the canvas into large squares.

As Jessie watched with Wright and Ellis, he laid out a neat stack of the trimmed canvas squares on the tailgate in lines. Turning to the others, he indicated the squares and said, "Rip a strip about a half-inch wide off one side of these pieces and put a good fistful of powder on them. Then trim off a length of fuse, six or eight inches long, and push one end into the powder."

"You're doing just what I was planning to, Ki," Jessie said as she watched Ki demonstrating how the edges of the canvas were to be folded over and circled with the fuse to form a makeshift bag. "I'll get busy tying the ends of the canvas together. How many do you think we'll need?"

"We'd better just keep working until we've used

up all the explosive," Ki said thoughtfully.

Jessie shot a quick glance at the quantity of fuse and powder. "There ought to be enough of everything to make at least eight bags, maybe more. One thing's sure. We'll certainly need as many as we've got materials to make."

None of them even bothered to count the bags that they produced during a busy quarter of an hour as a small but substantial pile of the filled makeshift canvas sacks rose on the wagon's tailgate. At last their materials ran out. Jessie turned to Ki and said, "I hope you've figured out a way to light these little bombs."

"I've been thinking of that ever since the idea occurred to me," Ki replied. "We've all got matches. What we can do is chop off the fuse five or six inches from the neck of the bags and carry a big lighted splinter of that sap-heavy pine to touch to the end of the fuse."

"It's crude but practical," Jessie said. "Let's go see if they work."

★

Chapter 9

"One thing we're going to have to do is to get all the Circle Star hands in from the range," Jessie said as they rode the last dozen yards up the slope. "Barstow's certainly going to try to get revenge if our plan works."

"That's not going to be as easy a job as it sounds, Jessie," Wright replied. "It'll take some hard riding."

"Then we'll just have to ride hard after we try our plan to discourage the squatters," she told him. "But we'll talk that over when we've seen how they act after getting the surprise we've got in store for them. I only hope it'll work."

"It's bound to work, Jessie!" Ki said. "The squatters won't really understand what's happening until it's too late, and that'll give us a good chance to disappear before they can figure out what to do."

By this time the little cavalcade had ridden up the rise and reined in just below its crest. Jessie went on. "We've got to spread out as we ride away and keep spread out as long as we're in rifle range. If we don't, and the squatters recognize us, we'll just be giving them easy targets."

"How far are we going to spread out?" Ellis asked.

"There isn't any way to tell," she said, twisting around in her saddle to face him. "Anything we'd plan to do now might be wrong later on. All that I've got in mind is for us to keep far enough apart so that if the squatters begin shooting at us . . ." Jessie broke off and shook her head. "I suppose I should've said *when* they start instead of *if*. As long as Pleas Barstow's telling them what to do they won't overlook or forgive."

"Isn't that borrowing more worry than we need to carry with us, Jessie?" Ki asked.

"Oh, I suppose it is, Ki," she replied. "But I still can't get it off my mind."

"Once we've done our job and ridden out, it might not be as easy as it sounds to keep the same space between us," Wright suggested.

"We won't have to bother about how we're spaced then, just as long as we don't get bunched up," Ki pointed out. His voice carried more assurance than it had earlier as he went on. "All we need to do is keep a good stretch of ground between each other. We won't have to be too careful, not after the squatters find out they've got some fires on their hands."

"That's right," Jessie said. "When we start now we'll be riding in the same direction that the man we glimpsed a few minutes ago was heading, to that flat space where they've got the big tent spread out. Ed, you keep right behind me, Ellis will be next, and Ki will be our rear guard."

"And all we have to do is keep apart?" Ellis asked.

Jessie nodded. "If our luck holds out, we'll be taking them by surprise, and if we get our fires started we'll be giving them something to worry about at the same time."

"Jessie's right," Ki put in. "Those men down on the flat will have their hands full once the tent starts going up."

"And I don't think any of us missed noticing that they've tethered their mounts a pretty fair space away," Wright added. "They wanted their horses far enough from the tent to give them plenty of working room when they begin raising it."

As the foreman fell silent Jessie said, "Now, the way we've figured things out, we ought to keep a pretty good lead on the bunch that'll likely take after us. Of course, I'm just guessing, but if they do, it's not too far to the first Circle Star grazing range where there'll be some of our own hands. They'll help us fight them off."

"It looks like to me that Jessie's made it real clear, so all of us understand what we need to do," Wright stated. "And these makeshift bombs won't hold up if they're handled too much, so we'd better get started."

Each of them clutched two of the makeshift pouches. The elongated bundles were filled with gunpowder and held together by lengths of fuse cord crisscrossed tightly around them. One end of the fuse cord extended from each bundle, ready to be touched with the flame of a match.

Jessie glanced at Ki, who made a small gesture to indicate that he was prepared to go. She turned back to Wright and nodded. He twisted his leg to tighten up his jeans and stuck a pair of matches in his mouth. Ellis followed suit. Jessie gripped her matches between her thumb and the palm of her hand, while Ki dropped his into one of the capacious pockets of his jacket.

Though Jessie was aware that their preparations fell short of perfection, she also knew that they were as well prepared as possible. She nudged Sun's flank with her boot heel, and as the palomino started ahead she pushed her foot more firmly into its stirrup. Following her example, they all kept the horses to a walk as they emerged from the shelter of the rise, but by this time the squatters were crowding up to the tent, too busy to notice the strange riders that were approaching.

All of the squatters, men and women alike,

were involved in getting the big stretch of canvas erected or watching it happen. Lumpy forms were now visible under what had been a flat spread of canvas moments earlier. The shapeless humps moving slowly ahead of a long narrow rippling bulge indicated that some of the workers involved in the tent-raising were starting to drag the tent's three big center poles into their places beneath the canvas.

Around the perimeter of the stretched-out tent there were other moving bulges. These marked the spots where more hidden workers were busy at the juncture of the top and the walls, lacing them together. A few men carrying coils of gleaming new rope had started walking across the stretched-out expanse of canvas. They were heading for the center of the big spread, getting ready to secure lasso loops to three wrist-thick iron shafts that had suddenly appeared along the tent's ridge. The short round stubs of metal protruded from the canvas at its top and marked the tops of its center poles.

Jessie gestured for her little band to space themselves a bit wider, and they started to spread out. Within a few moments they were riding as closely as possible to the edge of the big expanse of canvas.

There were numerous bulges now beneath the canvas, marking the locations of the men who would be the ones to insert the big spikes that topped the tent's main center poles in

101

the grommets fixed into the canvas along the ridgeline. Others were waiting to affix the side poles to the big tent's walls. All of them were waiting for the crucial moments when its raising would begin. Even the horsemen whose lariats would pull the center poles erect and raise the canvas looked a bit worried.

Pleas Barstow also looked anxious. He was pacing slowly around the tent's perimeter, calling some order or other every second or third step. Jessie had spotted him at once. She had been careful to stay several yards behind him, keeping a generous space between them.

Barstow drew his revolver from its holster and raised his voice to shout, "Don't forget, we all got to start at the same time now! Everybody get busy doing your job when you hear my shot! Let's get this damn tent up and not make no mistakes!"

Barstow swiveled around, running his eyes along the edges of the big span of canvas. Then he tilted the muzzle of his pistol to the sky and triggered off a shot. Ripples in the canvas started to appear as the men beneath it began lifting tent poles and tightening ropes.

Jessie had been watching with the others for the crucial moment to arrive, the moment when Barstow fired his shot. She waited until the humps that had been almost motionless under the spread-out canvas started moving. Knowing now where the hidden workers were when they began raising the tent poles, Jessie quickly guessed the distance and tossed her improvised bombs. They landed with low-pitched thunks near the center of the big canvas where the tent's main spinal line was growing taut. Almost immediately flickering flames began to spring up along the outstretched canvas roof.

Glancing ahead, Jessie saw that Wright was just tossing his bombs. They sailed several yards beyond the ones Jessie had tossed, dropping atop the canvas just a bit more than an arm's length from the point where the bulging figure of one of the tent-raising crew showed, plainly outlined. Fingers of fire began flickering around the bombs. There were a soft muffled explosions followed by thin threads of smoke from the small lines of reddish flame which started to spread at once, devouring the canvas.

Now Ki measured with his eyes the spot where his bombs should land. He tossed them quickly, for their fuses were getting dangerously short. The bombs landed and more bursts of flame quickly followed. Now as Jessie looked again along the ridge of the canvas expanse she saw that in addition to her successful throws, dancing tongues of flame were also rising and spreading from the spots where Ki and Wright had tossed their incendiary loads. Then Ellis made his throw, his bombs landing close to Ki's.

Within seconds the panic created by the first visible streaks of flame was spreading as fast as the blazes that were eating away the big stretch of canvas. The dancing lines of fire grew larger by the minute as the flames became more and more intense and continued to grow brighter. By this time the red tongues were spreading rapidly downward from the top of the tent. They became increasingly intense, brighter and hotter, for now the spreading flames had reached the second layer of the huge canvas spread.

From almost every point of the squatter settlement shouts were now rising in volume, not only from the squatters running to escape the streaks of flame, but also from those who still remained around the perimeter of the big expanse of canvas. Suddenly the three men who'd been below the tent's flattened peak broke through the blackened area where the first improvised firebombs had landed.

Once free, they began fighting their way through increasingly dense clouds of smoke as they tried to reach safety. So suddenly had the fires started to eat outward from the points on the canvas where they'd landed that many of the squatters who'd seen the blazes begin and grow, still stood frozen where they'd been standing to watch the tent-raising. None of them paid any attention to Jessie's little group.

More of the fleeing squatters were beginning to stream away from the blaze as its heat grew more intense. Most of them kept their eyes fixed over their shoulders on the flames that were dancing toward them as the fires continued to eat their way across the outspread canvas.

The onlookers, men and women alike, had been so stunned at the appearance of the first small tongues of flame that that all they could do was to stare in silence. Several minutes passed before shouts of encouragement began breaking the near silence that had followed when the shimmering blotches of fire first began to eat big holes in the canvas.

As the flames started shooting higher and their inroads on the canvas began to grow larger, the spectators at a distance from the spreading fire line still paid no attention to Jessie or to the men with her. Those who were streaming toward the blaze kept their eyes on the flames and on the bulges that marked the positions of the workers still invisible below the canvas.

But only a small handful of the spectators ran to help the endangered squatters. Even those who were a substantial distance from the fire were running away from it as though they might also be in danger of getting trapped. They ignored the stumbling figures now visible on the burning canvas, and ran toward the wagons and the small tents that had been pitched willy-nilly around the range.

Jessie and her little group left unnoticed and made their way back to the wagon. They said little. The sudden spreading fury of the fire had surprised them almost as greatly as it had surprised the squatters.

After untying Berle and sending him on his way toward the camp, they rode in silence until the burning tent was out of sight, all that marked its presence a red glow that broke the deep blue of the prairie's sky. At last Jessie spoke up.

"I wonder if the squatters are going to be fighting back at us, or if the fire will discourage them," she said, her voice thoughtful.

"That's something we'll just have to wait to find out," Ki replied. "But we've given them a message that might teach them a lesson."

"They're pretty badly spooked now," Jessie noted. "Our firebombs are teaching them it's not as easy as Pleas Barstow must've made it out to be to build a town on land that belongs to somebody else."

"What I'm wondering right now is if they're going to try getting revenge," Wright put in. "They won't think of us setting their tent afire to pay them back for trying to burn down the Circle Star main house the other night."

"Pleas Barstow looked to be a man who won't take a backward step without fighting," Ki said. "And he certainly won't be dragging his heels when somebody gets in between him and something he wants to do."

"That's the same way I figure him to be," Jessie agreed. "And when he makes his move for revenge against the Circle Star, we'll need to be ready to make sure that he doesn't take two steps instead of one."

"You think he'll do that right away?" Ki asked her.

"Of course he will!" Jessie replied instantly. "It'll take him quite a while to get his own bunch rounded up and ready to ride, but my guess is that as soon as the fire burns itself out he'll put in the rest of the day doing just that."

"To make a night attack?" Ki asked.

"Perhaps, but probably not tonight," Jessie replied. "My guess is that he'd be most apt to hit the Circle Star just before daybreak."

"Of course. They'd need some time to get ready," Ki decided. "Which means we'd better get what hands we've got out range-riding started toward the main house right away to be ready for him and his Galvanized Yankees."

"We're lucky to have as much daylight as we've got," Wright said. "But getting the hands in off the farthest range won't be easy, Jessie."

"It's going to be hard," Jessie agreed. She stopped. "Maybe it won't be as hard as it looks to be, though."

"I guess I don't follow you," Wright said.

"From where we are now, it'll be easy for you and Ki to divide up the range and warn the hands to be on the lookout tonight," she replied.

"And tell them to come in?" Wright frowned.

"No, indeed!" Jessie exclaimed. "Tell them to keep especially alert and to ride spread out. And be sure to tell them to use their guns when intruders begin to move to the sections

107

they're responsible for. I don't believe there'll be any rustling. My bet is that Barstow will tell his men to kill any steers or horses or riders they can. He'll be out for revenge, not to rustle cattle."

"We've got about six ranges where there'll be two hands," Wright said. "Don't you think I ought to get the extra hands started for the main house?"

"Yes, I'm sure we'll need them," Jessie said. "We're almost certain to be attacked by Barstow's men before tomorrow dawns."

★

Chapter 10

"I don't mind telling you, Miss Jessie, I was about the most surprised hand on the Circle Star when you asked me to dig out my long-gun and stand ready to give some cross fire to you in the main house." As he spoke, the grizzled cook was wiping his hands on his apron in the cookshack.

"I don't imagine your gun hand has much rust on it, Bridges," Jessie said with a smile.

"Well, now," he replied. "Even if I ain't let off a shot in a coon's age, I'd reckon my aim's near as good as it used to be. That's when your daddy was just getting the Circle Star in shape. Things was a lot rougher then than they are now, and he was having more'n his share of trouble with rustlers."

"You've been here on the Circle Star so long

that you're certainly no stranger to the sort of raiders that might try a surprise attack on us," she told him. "They're not rustlers, just really mean kinds of trash, but they've got plenty of guns and can really make things bad for us."

"And I reckon you got Ki and Wright out looking for 'em?"

"Of course," Jessie said. "Right now they're riding in a sweep to cover all the ranges where we've got herds grazing, but they ought to be back early tomorrow. In case they're not, and the squatters jump us, I thought about getting you to fill in for them until the others get here."

"Now, you know I'll do whatever you need me to, Miss Jessie," Bridges said. "But maybe you'd oughta tell me just what you got in mind."

"First of all," Jessie went on, "I'd like for you to pass the word to the hands' wives that their husbands will be staying out range-riding in case the squatters get really mean and try to kill our herds."

"I know just the kind of trash you're talking about," Bridges said. "The kind that've got gall enough to come on our range and potshoot our steers."

"They certainly would," Jessie assured him. "And there are so many men in that mangy outfit of Barstow's that they can do that and attack us here in the main house at the same time. All they've got to do is decide how they want to split up, and they can hit our herds on most any range about any time of day or night they choose."

"I hadn't looked at that way, but you're sure right," Bridges said. "And I hadn't figured on 'em hitting the houses where the hands live, too."

"Of course they would," she said soberly. "What bothers me most is that they're sure to do some rustling on the ranges where we hold our best market steers."

"And we wouldn't have much of a way to stop 'em," Bridges said.

"There's just one way I can figure out to do that," Jessie told him. "What I'd like for you to do is go rouse the wives and tell them that I'd be glad for them to come shelter in the main house. They'll be safe there, behind brick walls."

"That'll be easy," he answered. "Then I figure you'll want me to hole up in one of the vacant cabins where you and me can get them outlaws in a cross fire?"

"That's what I've got in mind," Jessie replied. "A lot of those newer cabin walls are board-built, but you've been at the Circle Star long enough to know which cabins are solid and which aren't."

Bridges nodded his head. "I know the kind you mean. The old ones'll stop most anything but a cannonball. You can bet there ain't going to be no rifle bullet going through 'em."

"Then you pick out a cabin for yourself," Jessie said. "One of the old adobe ones that'll give you clear shots in the direction of the main house,

111

because that's bound to be their first target. I'll leave that up to you."

"Now, I can tell you're getting all fretted up, Miss Jessie," Bridges said. "And there ain't no reason to do that. This ain't the first time outlaws has tried to chouse us here on our home grounds. And I know you can handle a rifle better'n most men, including me."

"I'm not so sure about that," Jessie replied. "More than once I've watched you punch a bull's-eye in a target five straight rounds when the hands were having a friendly shoot-off."

"Well, I just wish I was as good a shot as you are, but I know better, Miss Jessie. When the younger hands started shooting better than me, I decided I'd best turn to cooking, and I ain't about to do no bragging."

"If we're lucky, there won't be too many good shots among the squatters," Jessie said. "I don't know how many of the men that Barstow calls his Galvanized Yankees will be in the bunch that's likely to take us on here, but at least we'll have time to get ready to greet them."

"Why, it won't matter a whole lot how many of them squatters we can look for, Miss Jessie," Bridges assured her. "All we got to do is give 'em enough what-for with hot lead, and you can bet your bottom dollar they won't stay around too long."

"I hope you've called the turn," Jessie replied. "But right now we've been using up a lot of time that might be put to better use. I need to hurry back to the main house and be getting ready myself."

There was no sign of an attack by the squatters while Jessie was attending to making the hands' wives as comfortable as possible. She accepted the offers of the two younger women who volunteered to join her in defending the sprawling main house. After Jessie gave them rifles and ammunition from the racks in the basement, she placed one of the young women in a corner bedroom on the second floor, above the trail, overlooking it. The other she positioned at a basement window just above ground level.

"You've only got one thing to be careful about," she told each of them in turn. "And that's making yourself a target. Just don't go near a window while your lamp's lighted. You'll need to break out a window-glass. All we have to do is get through the night. Our men will be coming in off the range right before dawn."

"You mean the whole outfit?" one of the women asked.

"Of course not," Jessie replied. "Just those who're the best shots. Most likely they'll get here one or two at a time. I don't imagine the squatters will hit us until daybreak, and my guess is that they'll be bunched up. Before you let off a shot, just be sure you've got one of them in your sights instead of one of our own hands."

113

"Don't worry, Jessie," the woman assured her. "We ought to be able to tell the difference between them and our own men, even if it's still dark. We won't shoot at anybody but the squatters."

Jessie nodded. "I know you'll be careful in picking your targets if those squatters make a shooting run at us. So now about all we can do is wait."

Jessie was in the kitchen brewing coffee when the first faint thunking of horses' hooves reached her ears. Picking up her rifle, she stepped to the window.

A faint tint of gold had started to lighten the eastern sky, announcing the oncoming sunrise, but Jessie could see at a glance that another half hour or more remained before the first real daylight arrived. She stood in silent attentiveness for a moment until she was sure that her ears weren't deceiving her. Then, as the steadily louder thud of hoofbeats assured her that the squatters were on their way, she moved out the back door and crouched on a low step of the rear stairs between the adobe balustrade and the wall, ready to greet the approaching squatters with their first surprise.

Jessie was not impatient. She knew that she'd need to allow for some time to pass in order to accustom her eyes to the darkness. She kept her cover, and when the first pair of attacking riders came within earshot, tilted the muzzle of her

Winchester level with her shoulder and triggered off a shot.

Thumps of threshing hooves and raised voices followed the report of the reverberation of her warning shot. Raising her voice without breaking her cover, Jessie called out, "I'll give you men a chance to turn around and go back to where you came from! This is the only warning you'll get! Now, turn your horses and move off!"

A rifle barked from the oncoming squatters, and another slug followed almost at once. Both bullets whistled well above Jessie's head and thunked into the thick wall of the main house. Though Jessie could not yet see the oncoming squatters clearly, vague outlines of movement had now become visible through the darkness, and she fired at the nearest, but with no success.

Then, when the muzzle-blast of more shots from the squatters broke the gloom, Jessie lowered her Winchester's muzzle a bit and loosed a second shot. She did not wait to see if her bullet had hit or missed, but fired again as quickly as she could lever a fresh shell into the rifle's breech. The response from the oncoming riders was the high-pitched neighing of a wounded horse and another few moments of thudding hooves on the narrow pathway.

Jessie wasted no time levering a fresh round into her rifle's breech. Her next reply to the raiding outlaws came swiftly, two shots loosed as fast as she could get fresh rounds into the breech. Another snort of a horse in pain broke the darkness; this time it was much louder than the first.

From one of the second-floor windows of the big house a flash of muzzle-blast and the crisp crack of a rifle sounded. It was followed by a yell and the high-pitched neighing of still another wounded horse. New shouts began sounding from the attacking squatters. For the most part the squatters' words were not intelligible, but the thudding of hooves from their horses grew steadily louder and closer.

Jessie took advantage of the moments to slip fresh shells into the magazine of her Winchester. Just as she was inserting the final round a thudding of hooves filled the darkness and she looked up, straining her eyes to pierce its shroud. Dimly, she saw the half-visible forms of several riders gaining speed as they got closer to the main house and vanished behind the trail's curve sweeping toward the cabins of the Circle Star's hands.

Even before the invading squatters had started riding past her, Jessie was bringing up the Winchester. She fanned the gun's muzzle to get the final horseman in her sights, but before she could take a bead the rider had swept beyond her. Jessie started lowering the barrel of her rifle, but stopped, allowing it to droop when for the second time the clopping of hooves reached her ears.

Her eyes had finally gotten their night vision

while she was waiting, and she fanned the Winchester's muzzle to the next rider and took quick aim before triggering off her shot. The slug from her rifle went to its target. The horseman's rifle dropped from his hands as her bullet took him squarely between his shoulders.

He jerked back in his saddle as his rifle clattered on the trail's hard-packed ground and held himself erect for a moment, trying to keep in his saddle, then sagged and slipped over the horse's withers to the ground to lie in a motionless, crumpled heap.

After seeing the rider starting to crumple, Jessie began moving. She took two steps along the balustrade and crouched behind it while she was levering another shell into the chamber of her Winchester. Then she rose cautiously, kneeling on the top stair-step, to wait for another target.

Her wait was short. Another slowly moving horseman appeared in the gloom, and she swiveled her Winchester's muzzle to get him in her sights. Shifting to the new point of aim, Jessie waited only a few seconds for the oncoming raider to appear.

When he finally did, a moving target barely visible in the half-light, Jessie shifted to get a bead on him and fired again. Like the man before him, the horseman reared back in his saddle and slid from his moving horse over its rump, to lie with the stillness in an awkward sprawl.

Suddenly the thunking hoofbeats began to fade

instead of coming closer. Loud shouts, most of them unintelligible, were coming from the throats of the attacking squatters. Now Jessie could see six or eight horsemen through the darkness, milling around on and beside the trail. At the same time the dull clomping of other hoofbeats told her that there were still more men coming.

Then the heavier reverberations of a shot beyond the big house told her that either another group of night riders or the survivors who'd launched the attack on the big house had come into Bridges's view. A second shot followed, and now Jessie got a quickly passing glimpse of a horseman speeding past her. Although there were no longer any riders visible, the thudding hoofbeats were still loud.

Now a shot sounded from the scattered dottings of the small cabins beyond the main house. The high-pitched squeal of pain from a horse cut the air before a second shot from the same source brought a dying neigh from the animal. It was followed by a weakened whinny, and before it died away she heard a dulled thud and an unintelligible shout from its rider. Jessie started toward the noises, but before she could break her scanty cover as she reached the corner of the big building, a man whose figure she could hardly make out ran past her and disappeared in the darkness beyond the house's corner.

Only a moment passed before the thudding hoofbeats broke the sudden silence again, and

Jessie stopped short, peering around as she tried to pierce the veil of blackness. Then she turned back to the shelter she'd just stepped away from, waiting just long enough to give her a fleeting second look at the rifleman before dropping behind the stair wall again.

Her guess or hunch proved its merit, for again a shot cracked and a bullet whistled above her head and buried itself in the wall, just as the earlier shot had. Now that Jessie knew the location of the shootist, she knew just where to stop the fanning of her rifle. Switching its muzzle quickly, Jessie waited for the attacking rifleman to show himself again.

When he appeared, his weapon already moving to cover her sheltered spot, Jessie triggered off her shot first. In her haste, she'd not taken time to seat her rifle butt firmly and the recoil of her rifle knocked her off her feet.

She did not try to rise at once, but the lack of a shot in reply to her last one told her that her slug had sailed true and that it was the man's dying reflex in closing on the trigger of his rifle that had discharged the weapon as Jessie's hot lead found its intended target. Her bullet had thrown the attacker backward from his mount, and he'd been landing on the ground as his finger closed on his rifle's trigger.

Then, even before she was moving to get back on her feet, Jessie heard the loud flat reverberations from Bridges's rifle, which told their own story. In spite of the resistance she and her companions had made, at least a few of the night riders were still around to follow up their first swift attack.

For a few moments there was nothing but silence broken by a few loud shouts from the attackers. They lasted for only a moment before the distant drumming sounds of hoofbeats from the darkness in the near distance told Jessie that the squatters were not accepting defeat. Faint shouts rose again as the thudding of horses' hooves grew from a whisper to their peak as they started up the incline to resume their attack on the main house.

This time the diminished number of squatters was moving more slowly, for their already tired mounts were facing an uphill grade as well as the muzzles of the rifles from the newly arriving Circle Star hands. The hoofbeat thuds on the upslope were more widely spaced, and the menacing shouts no longer broke the brightening darkness as a shining moon silhouetted the attackers.

Jessie swiveled her rifle along the course followed by one of the outlaws and held her rifle's muzzle steady as she triggered off her shot. Two other shots followed from the oncoming riders before her target had tumbled off his mount. By this time the remaining defenders of the big house had disappeared in the gloom.

Now, shouts arose from the attackers, who were again drawing closer to the main house. Suddenly the rider in the saddle of the lead horse realized that he was leading his band into a hornet's nest. He yanked at the reins of his mount to turn it away from the big house, and was at once swallowed by the night's dark curtain.

When Jessie saw the squatters reining away she got a clear glimpse of one of them, and swung her rifle's muzzle to let off a quick round. It missed, for now the leader had moved away by turning off the beaten path, and the others were following him.

She tried to get one of the other galloping riders in her sights, but before she succeeded he'd already reached the side of the road. She realized then that he'd been looking for the spot where it dipped sharply into the big meadow beside the trail.

Now Jessie heard the loud yell he loosed as he reined away from the main building to join the retreat of the other squatters. She swiveled again, but before she could swing around and bring up her Winchester to get him in her sights, he was lost in the darkness.

Suddenly nothing except the steadily diminishing thunking of hoofbeats broke the gloom. In another few minutes only silence reigned around the main house of the Circle Star.

★

Chapter 11

"It's already a bad situation, Ki," Jessie said.

As soon as they'd finished breakfast, she and Ki had started riding wide sweeps along the stretch of range between the Circle Star's main house and the section of its range where the squatters had settled. Several times their zigzag courses had brought them fairly close together at the end of one of their courses, but this was the first time they'd met at easy speaking distance.

Jessie went on. "Anything we might do trying to cure it is only likely to make things worse, and I don't want to call any men in off the range again. If the Circle Star wasn't so sprawled out, we could go to the nearest ranches and ask for help, but that would mean losing at least two days, maybe three or four."

"Yes, I can see that," Ki agreed after a moment of thoughtful silence. "But you were right to send the hands back to the ranges after breakfast. I don't think Barstow's bunch will be foolish enough to attack us again."

"Let's ride another sweep or two, then," Jessie went on. "Then we'll see about taking the squatters' bodies back to their camp."

"There's not any reason for you to do a job like that," Ki told her. "Let me or one of the hands take care of it."

"I have a very good reason for wanting to do that myself, Ki," Jessie told him. "It's to impress on Barstow the idea that we're going to drive him and his squatters off Circle Star range as quickly as we can."

"Maybe I shouldn't ask you this, Jessie, but do you actually think that Barstow's going to be softened up just by seeing a couple of bodies? He knows that he's got at least three or four times as many squatters to back him up as we've got ranch hands."

"Of course he does," Jessie said. "But we're going to find a way get him off Circle Star land in spite of that bunch of killers he's brought with him, the ones he calls his Galvanized Yankees."

Ki waited for a moment for Jessie to continue, and when she said nothing more he suggested, "If you've got an idea of some sort, I'd like to hear it."

"I'm just beginning to think it through," Jessie told him. "Getting rid of Barstow and his squatters is something that's—well, I suppose the easiest way to put it is to say it's a duty we've got to do, to keep us and other ranchers from being nibbled away."

"And you intend to do your part," Ki said. "How do you plan to begin?"

"Let me do a little bit more thinking, Ki," Jessie replied.

"If it'll help you any, I'll tell you what I'm thinking about right now," Ki said. "We've got to face Barstow down, Jessie."

"Of course we do. And without wasting any time."

"It's either bluff him or fight him," Ki said. "And we don't have enough hands to risk stirring up a ruckus with that crowd he's got."

"I feel the same way," Jessie answered quickly. "And we've also got to remember that Barstow's not a man to listen to anybody. He wants his way all the time."

"Perhaps he won't after we've done the little chore I've been thinking about," Ki told her. "It popped into my mind while you were talking, and we'll want one of the hands to go along and give us some help. I've got Ed Wright in mind if you don't have anything special for him to do."

"Nothing that can't wait," Jessie assured Ki. "And if you need Bridges, count on him, too. Even if your plan doesn't have any effect on Barstow, it might influence some of the squatters and even turn them away."

"That's what I've been figuring," Ki said.

"Let's talk about it on the way back to the big house," she suggested. "I don't know about you, but I'm hungry."

By the time Jessie and Ki and Wright had started for the section of range being occupied by the squatters, the sun was well past its zenith. Wright had insisted on leading the horse he and Ki had agreed would be the easiest to handle with the load that had to be carried. Lashed across the animal's back were the bodies of the two dead squatters they'd found on the Circle Star range.

Though they had only a relatively short ride, by the time they'd reached the edge of the section Barstow was claiming, the day was moving toward a close, the bottom of the sun's rim hanging only a hand's span above the horizon. When a stretch of sagging fence line loomed ahead of them, Jessie turned to Wright.

"I see that they've cut our line fence," she said. "More than likely they did that when they rode out on their raid last night."

"Oh, I'd say it was a pretty sure thing," Wright agreed. "And I don't know what your idea is about fixing it, Jessie, but unless we've got some other kind of job like we had to take care of last night, I'll send a couple of hands up here tomorrow to mend it."

"Let's wait to make any more plans until we see how we come out in our palaver with Barstow,"

Ki said. "And that's not going to be very far off, because unless I miss my bet that's Barstow and some of his Galvanized Yankees riding in our direction right now."

"I'm sure we won't be able to change his mind about anything," Jessie told him. "But we've got to try. If we let the squatters begin to build their new town on that upper section of range, they're going to get the idea that we won't object to them doing just about anything they choose to. Including killing some of our steers when they need to keep meat on their tables. To say nothing of them starting to build a shanty or even a full-sized house anywhere else on Circle Star land wherever they please."

"I'd say the worst thing they've done is that foolish night raid they tried. If it hadn't been for the hands' wives, we'd have had a lot bigger job than we did fighting them off. Barstow must've told those those raiders to stage a real shootout."

"Not that they didn't," Jessie reminded them. "Even if we don't have a bit of proof that those Galvanized Yankees attacked us on Pleas Barstow's orders."

By the time Jessie and Ki and Wright finished their brief exchanges, they were almost within hailing distance of the oncoming riders. There were four of them, riding in a scattered group with Barstow a bit in the lead. Before they'd reached easy speaking distance Jessie reined in, forcing the squatter group to ride the small extra distance to where she'd halted.

"I reckon we both had the same idea," Barstow said when he'd motioned for his companions to stay and continued advancing alone to meet Jessie's small party. She did not greet him, but gestured for Ki and Wright to stay close.

"So it seems," Jessie replied. Her voice was cold as she went on. "But at first I had the idea that it was too much to expect a *gaucho* like you to face someone who'd been attacked on a peaceful ranch in the darkness."

Barstow opened his mouth as though he was going to protest Jessie's designation of him as a *gaucho,* a third-class ranch hand. Then he ignored the studied insult and protested, "Now, just hold on a minute, Miss Starbuck. That little fracas some of the squatters rode out on last night wasn't any of my doing."

Wright lifted himself in his stirrups before Jessie could reply, but she waved to him to settle down. Then she turned back to Barstow and asked, "If that's the case, which I very much doubt, why didn't you stop them?"

"Because I didn't even know there'd been any night riders until they started coming back," Barstow replied. "I heard 'em riding in, hooting and yelling, and went out to see what it was all about. And by the time I'd got to the bottom of what them fools had done, it was just too late to do anything about it."

"I don't consider your explanation at all

convincing," Jessie replied. "But you can prove that you meant what you said by getting your squatters together and moving them off my range. After they've packed up and I've seen them leaving, I'll accept your regrets."

"Now, just hold up a minute!" Barstow exclaimed. "I didn't come all this way from up in the far north corner of the Panhandle guiding these land-hunters just to turn around and guide 'em back!"

"I don't expect you to guide them back to where you started from," Jessie went on. "I just want them far enough away to keep them from causing any more trouble on the Circle Star."

"How far would you figure that to be?" Barstow said. "I know that every man-jack of those Galvanized Yankees in that bunch with me is figuring on settling down in Texas."

"I'm not trying to give you orders," Jessie answered. "But there's plenty of good rangeland to the north in New Mexico and Colorado just waiting to be claimed."

For several moments Barstow did not reply. Then he said, "I don't figure that'd suit these folks. They want to be someplace where it don't snow in the wintertime and and rains enough to keep grazing land green."

Although Jessie now saw that it was time for her to object, she managed to keep her voice level as she said, "There's no such thing as a rancher's heaven."

"Well, you got—" he began.

Jessie cut him off short. "Now, I'm certainly not going to listen to your next suggestion, because I'm quite sure it's your idea to propose that I sell part of the Circle Star to those people, and that's the furthest thing from my plans."

"You got a lot more land than anybody's got a right to!" Barstow exploded. He was fast losing control of his voice as well as his temper. His face was flushed and he was almost shouting as he replied to Jessie.

"That's where you're wrong," she answered, still keeping her voice under control. "There are plenty of ranchers who work more land than I do. And there are a lot who have less. But there's not one who won't fight to keep what they've earned."

Barstow had his mouth open to reply to Jessie when his eyes fell on the two dead men lashed on the horse. "You killed some of my men to boot! One of my best hands and one of the Galvanized Yankees! And that's something I'll sure make you pay for!"

"I'm afraid you've got your ideas turned backward," Jessie said coolly. "Your men were raiding my ranch when they were killed. Perhaps they weren't rustlers, but they were certainly acting like they were." Turning to Ki she went on. "Cut the rope holding the bodies on the horse, Ki. We'll leave it up to Barstow and his crew to bury them."

Barstow opened his mouth to reply, but the

angry words he'd intended to pour out on Jessie's little group died unuttered in his throat. Ki had already taken out his clasp-knife while toeing his mount back, and the distance between him and the horse bearing the bodies was rapidly closing.

Barstow glanced at Jessie, and his cattleman's eyes told him that he could not reach Ki in time to stop him. He could only let his half-lifted reins go slack and watch while Ki reined in beside the horse and leaned forward in his saddle to reach the steed and its grisly burden. One quick slash of the razor-sharp blade severed the rope, and the death-distorted and stiffened corpses dropped to the ground below the horse.

Barstow opened his mouth to protest, but Ki grabbed the reins of the horse and started back to join Jessie and Wright. Jessie touched Sun's reins and started back in the direction of the Circle Star's main house with her little entourage following her.

They'd covered only a short distance when Jessie turned to look back over her shoulder. Barstow was still in his saddle beside the bodies, his horse tossing its head as though it wanted to move away from the grisly scene. Then Barstow reined away, dug his boot heels into his mount's flanks and started at a gallop in the direction of the squatters' camp.

★

Chapter 12

"I'm glad to see him go," Jessie said as they continued to ride. "And I certainly don't intend to let his squatters settle in just as though they already own this section of the Circle Star. We'll simply have to figure out a way to get enough men here to stop them."

"We're going to need more time than we've got," Wright said. "We can't get our men in from the ranges before Barstow trots the squatters out for a showdown. I've been trying to think of a way to get them in off the range in time, but I haven't come up with one."

"Neither have I," Ki said. "We'd be too badly outnumbered to turn them away, especially if he comes back with a lot of his Galvanized Yankees."

"I've been trying to think of a way to even up

those odds," Jessie said. "And I've finally gotten an idea. I hope it works out right, because if it does, we'll more than likely be rid of the squatters."

"If you've got a plan, let's hear it, Jessie," Ki suggested. "We need to move as fast as we can. We don't have a lot of time left before Barstow's going to be back with all his men, and we can be sure that includes his Galvanized Yankees."

"He can't get all of them together in just an hour or two," Jessie stated. "He's got to do a bit of talking to them, and likely, to the squatters as well. That's going to take some time. We're only a half-hour ride from the Circle Star, and the answer to our problem just might be in the main-house basement."

Both Ki and Wright turned to look at Jessie with puzzled frowns on their faces. At last Ki said, "I can't think of anything down there that would help us. Just easy chairs and a table or two in the part we use."

"What I'm talking about is in the big storage room," Jessie said. "You ought to remember what's in there."

For a moment Ki did not reply. Then he said, "If I'm not mistaken, Jessie, that storage room just has a few pieces of discarded furniture in it. There are some crates and boxes down there that've been gathering dust for a long time, so long that I don't even remember what's in them."

"It's the crates and boxes I'm thinking about,

Ki," she told him. "Have you forgotten General Ripley's last visit?"

"Of course not," Ki replied. "Although, since it was such a long time back, I remember you were here, taking your school vacation. But I still don't . . ." Suddenly he paused and stared silently at Jessie.

"I see you've finally remembered General Ripley's boxes," she said. "I'm talking about the crates he left when he had to leave. They were supposed to be picked up and carried somewhere else by the army squad he'd been waiting for."

"But that squad never got here," Ki reminded her. "Then the general and the soldiers with him were killed in that bad train wreck on his way back East."

"I remember," Jessie said. "Alex waited for a while, then sent a letter to army headquarters, but he never did get an answer. Nobody back East seemed interested in answering his letter, and as for me—well, that wasn't too long before Alex was killed."

"Yes, I remember all that," Ki replied. "You came back here after that to take charge of the Starbuck properties."

"And it didn't take me long to learn what a job it was," she went on. "I was lucky you were there to help me. But later on I found that I had so many things to do, I simply forgot that the army's boxes were among the other boxes and crates that were in the basement."

"That's easy to understand," Ki said. "I don't suppose there's anybody here on the ranch except you or me who ever goes down to the basement."

"Of course not," Jessie agreed. "I've got too many sad memories of most of the old chairs and settees and the—well, the junk that's accumulated down there—to go into that part of the basement."

Wright had been following the conversation between Jessie and Ki, a puzzled frown crinkling his brow. Now he said, "I don't mean to butt in on you and Ki, Jessie. But someplace when you and Ki begun talking, I sort of got lost."

"We can fill in the chinks for you on our way back to the main house," Jessie told him. "It won't take very long to do that. Because if what I've got in mind is going to turn out the way I want it to, we'll have a lot of jobs to take care of after we get there."

Jessie followed Ki's example, lifting her lantern above her head, as they passed from the wine cellar to the basement's first storage room and entered the dark chamber that adjoined it. With both lanterns aglow they could see the mishmash of small boxes and bundles and cloth-draped chairs standing in dusty humps around the half-filled room.

"It's not this room, Ki," she said. "We've got to go straight on back to the big storage closet at the end. There are two more doors in that far wall.

One of them has a padlock on it. That's the one we're interested in."

"You've got the key of course?" Ki asked.

"I've brought the key ring along," Jessie answered. "It has five or six keys on it. It won't take long or be hard to try them until we find the right one."

They reached the oversized door and Jessie tried three or four of the keys before the lock clicked. She pushed the door, but it did not yield until Ki bent to thunk with his shoulder on the heavy portal. It resisted for a moment, then opened a crack and stuck. Ki stepped back a half pace and brought up his foot to kick the door. This time it creaked and opened grudgingly to reveal a midnight blackness beyond the aperture.

Jessie stepped up with her lantern candle raised as high as possible in the low-ceilinged basement. Now they could see several slatted crates and a number of boxes. Neither the crates nor the boxes appeared to be very large, though it was next to impossible for them to judge the true bulk of any of the individual containers in the flickering glow shed by their candles.

"This is what we're looking for," she said. "I'm sure they're the ones General Ripley was talking about. But I don't think they're too heavy for us to carry. Let's try lifting a few and find out."

For the next few minutes Jessie and Ki were busy experimenting with both the large crates and the smaller boxes. To their surprise, the canvas-shrouded crates and the smaller wooden boxes were almost uniform in weight despite the differences in their size. After they'd finished their testing, Jessie turned to Ki and nodded.

"Moving them won't be easy. But we'd better get them into the wine cellar. There's a brick floor in there, so we won't raise any dust when we move around."

"You're right, it won't be easy," Ki agreed. "But you're also right about the dust."

"There aren't too many boxes," she said. "And I don't think that even the bigger crates are so heavy that we'd waste much time moving them into the wine cellar."

"We'll manage," Ki agreed. "And if we're going to move the boxes we'd better get started."

Between lifting the least heavy of the boxes and carrying them to the wine cellar, then pushing the largest of the remaining sturdy crates into the cellar over areas of hard-crusted soil, they busied themselves getting all the crates as well as the half-dozen remaining small but heavy boxes out of the storage closet. The bricked floor in the cellar simplified their job of moving the boxes around by giving them lots of stability underfoot.

"I'd say the worst of our jobs is done," Jessie told Ki after they'd moved all the boxes and crates. "Now that we've finished it, let's don't waste any time. We need a crowbar to open these boxes, and—"

"No, we don't," Ki broke in. "I can chip away the wood around the nails. It won't take much time."

Ki had slipped his razor-sharp dagger from its arm sheath as he was speaking. Now he began chipping away the wood around the nails at top of one of the crates. After he'd finished he thrust the blade between the top and side of one of the crates and pressed the knife handle firmly but slowly.

At first the small crack widened grudgingly, but within a few moments Ki saw that it was possible to slide his fingers into the crevice his efforts had opened. Sheathing his knife, Ki wrenched away the nailed sides, which were only short lengths of plank. He tossed the debris aside as Jessie stepped closer to the elongated box to help him.

Their joint efforts soon removed the top and sides of the box, revealing an oily cloth, and when the cloth was removed they could see a large cylinder of brass.

Jessie exclaimed, "That's it, Ki! It's one end of the barrel of that gun General Ripley was sent here to test! It's called a Gatling gun. That's why he came here, because Father had such a lot of range where nobody was likely to watch the testing," Jessie added. "I remember going to one of the tests with Father, and how fast the gun worked."

"And that's all you can remember?" Ki asked.

"I don't really remember much about it," Jessie replied. "But don't forget, I was just a girl then."

"Of course," Ki said. "Try to remember what you did hear and what you saw when you watched the gun being tried out."

"Well, I'm sure it's got some more pieces. And there's something like a brass hatbox on the top and a swiveling thing on the bottom and it doesn't have a trigger. There's a crank on one side, and you can swing the gun from one side to the other while you're firing it. I remember that much of the testing, but not much more."

"What you're really saying is that that crank fires the gun when it's being swiveled from side to side while you're shooting," Ki suggested.

"I suppose you could put it that way," Jessie said. "I'm just trying to recall exactly what happened the time I went with Alex and the general to watch the gun being tried out. I suppose we'll have to take it out and see if we can manage to put it together so it'll work."

"I don't believe we'll have too much trouble doing that," Ki told her. "We'll just have to figure out which part goes where, unless there's some sort of instruction sheet tucked away in one of these boxes."

"More than likely there is," Jessie assured him.

They bent over to find room to get their hands locked around the long brass cylinder. Though it made a heavy load, they managed to lift the heavy brass cylinder from its box. They deposited the cylinder on the floor and stood looking at it.

"If I can trust my memory," Jessie said, "this

big brass cylinder is the barrel. It fits into that U-shaped piece and the U-shaped piece goes on top of that big block of wood."

Ki had begun positioning the brass pieces on the floor in their proper places while Jessie studied the remaining hardware. He could see now how the shape of each piece fitted, and reached for the wooden base to begin assembling the gun.

He said, "I'm getting the idea now, Jessie. The big circular piece that reminds me of a gypsy's tambourine without any bottom, swivels around from one side to the other. Then, when the gun barrel's fixed into the U-shaped piece it'll move up and down. Does that make sense to you?"

After a moment of thought, Jessie said, "It does in a way, but there's more than that to the gun, Ki. The barrel goes into the top of that U-shaped piece you were talking about. One of those big heavy circular pieces holds the ammunition, and somewhere in these pieces is the crank that really makes the gun shoot."

Ki nodded. "But I can see that it's not complete. Let's look in these other boxes."

Their search was quick and rewarding. By matching bolt ends with the studs in each group, they had the gun assembled in a very short time. Jessie stepped back to look at it, and Ki moved to her side.

"That's just how I remember the gun looking," she told Ki. "And I also remembered that those small boxes are filled with ammunition for it, and the big thick circular brass pieces hold the shells it fires."

"Then we've got everything we need to try the gun out," Ki said. "Let's get Ed Wright to bring us a wagon. We'll go to one of the ranges where there aren't any grazing steers and see how it shoots."

★

Chapter 13

"Are we sure now that everything's fixed for us to have a try at shooting the Gatling gun?" Jessie asked as Ki and Wright got to their feet and dusted off their trouser legs.

"I imagine we're as ready as we'll ever be," Wright said. "We've gone through all that mess of papers in the box the gun was in, and did what they said to do when we were putting the pieces together, so we ought to know what to do and when."

"I'd say it's fixed as much as we can do it without wasting a lot more time," Ki replied. "But we're still not sure it's perfect."

"Perfect or not, we'd better get on with trying it out," Jessie replied. "It's the only way we'll ever learn what to do and what not to do."

They were on a section of the Circle Star's range that had a long gentle upslope and held no grazing steers. Ki and Wright had just finished driving sturdy inward-slanting stakes on all four sides of the Gatling gun's base to keep it anchored firmly in firing position.

Jessie had chosen this isolated section of the sprawling ranch for their test of the weapon because it was one of the sections nearest the main house and because it was not a level range. A broad and deep valley dipped down at a wide slant on one side of the stretch of prairie, while on the other side the terrain was broken by the rise of the valley's wall.

"Who's going to be first to shoot, then?" Ki asked.

"Well, I've never fired a gun like this one," Jessie said. Looking from one of her companions to the other, she added, "But I don't suppose any of us have."

"Why don't you go first," Wright suggested.

Ki nodded his approval.

Jessie smiled. "You'd better get behind me where you'll be safe, and we'll see if I can hit the side of that bluff up ahead."

While Ki and Wright moved behind her, Jessie dropped to her knees behind the Gatling gun. She bent forward, testing the big gunsight, then turned to say over her shoulder, "I'd better get used to sighting this gun before I try to hit a target with it."

Turning back to the weapon, she lowered her head until her eyes were almost level with the gun barrel. Jessie swiveled the gun from side to side and up and down, watching the clump of mesquite brush forty or fifty yards away that she'd chosen for a target. Only a moment was required for her to center the brush through the circular opening in the doughnut-shaped ammunition drum fitted on top of the barrel.

Clutching the weapon's butt with her left hand, Jessie instinctivly extended her right hand in search of a trigger, but found none. Remembering that the Gatling gun was triggerless, she moved her hand to grasp the knob of the crank that protruded from the side of the gun's back, almost a foot from the ammunition drum. Then she began turning the crank.

None of the trio was prepared for the metallic chatter of shots that followed. The gun barrel quivered and a constant ear-bursting *rat-tat-tat* filled the air. The doughnut-shaped brass ammunition drum rising from the rear of the gun's barrel was quivering, and through the hole in the drum's center Jessie could see the shining trail of a shallow arc of glistening brass bullets speeding from the muzzle to their target.

Jessie released the crank after a few moments and pressed her hands against her ears, trying to stop the ringing echo of the noise that had ended as soon as she stopped turning the crank. At first none of the trio looked in the direction in which the Gatling gun had been firing. When Jessie got to her feet and turned to gaze at her target, all she could do was to gasp and point.

Ki's and Wright's gulps of surprise were louder than Jessie's. The stand of mesquite brush had been taller than a standing man's head. Now the big growth had vanished almost completely, leaving only a scattered covering of bark bits and small pieces of branches on the ground around it.

Wright was the first to speak. His awed tone sounded loud in the silence that followed their inspection of the devastated mesquite stand as he said, "Now, I'd call that some kind of shooting! Why, I don't ever recall seeing a gun that cut down brush till you can't even tell it used to be there."

Jessie nodded as she told her companions, "You know, I've fired a pretty fair number of rifles and pistols, but I don't recall ever having seen a gun that does what this one just did. It's noisy as all get-out, but it never recoils backward. All it does is shiver and shake like it's got a bad case of the ague."

"I hope we're not fooling ourselves," Ki said. "We don't know how many of the men have ever seen anything like this gun before. We never have, but there's no way of knowing whether or not it's going to spook them."

"Oh, I imagine that a pretty good lot of them have seen a Gatling gun," Jessie said thoughtfully.

"Especially Barstow's Galvanized Yankees. But it won't take long for those who haven't seen one to find out what they're up against."

"Then let's get back to the main house," Ki suggested. "It won't take long for us to anchor that Gatling gun in a wagon bed. After that's done, we can take off for the squatters' camp and give them a chance to find out what it can do."

Just below the crest of the rise that concealed the shallow valley beyond, Jessie spurred up to the wagon. Ki was in the seat. Behind him the brass of the Gatling gun's barrel glinted like gold in the mid-morning sunshine.

Jessie motioned for Ki to pull up as she reined in her own mount and Wright touched the reins of his mount to shorten the distance between them. While he was moving toward her, Jessie saw the shining brass gun in its improvised mount, the dozen thick circular magazines for the weapon in its bed also reflecting the gun's golden hue. She shook her head, her expression showing the surprise she felt at their unexpected good luck, then turned back to face Wright, who was reining in beside the wagon.

"Let's just wait here a minute," she said, "and make sure that all of us are ready."

"Don't you think we'd better cover that gun with a piece of canvas, Jessie?" Ki asked. "There's no use in showing our ace in the hole right from the start."

"Of course we need to cover it," she agreed. "You can use that big piece of canvas just behind the wagon seat. You take care of the gun and make sure everything else is in place. The squatters don't seem to have noticed us yet, so you've got plenty of time."

"I'll handle that little job," Ki replied.

"We'll have the best of them from the start if we can take them by surprise," Jessie went on. "And at this time of the day they'll be busy getting ready for their noon meal."

"That means it's going to take a while for all of them to get outside at this time of day, Jessie," Ki observed. "But once we let off a few rounds they'll come running."

Ki began covering the Gatling gun with a large piece of the canvas.

"We'll split up just before we reach the rim of this rise." Jessie said. "Ed, you'll go left, I'll go to the right, and Ki can keep the wagon going straight ahead for a while longer."

"It'd sure help a lot if we knew how Barstow's going to act," Wright observed.

"All we can do is guess at that," Jessie replied. "I'm betting that when they see us, the squatters will likely start this way. That's when we'll loose off a string of shots from the Gatling gun over their heads."

"You think that's going to stop them, Jessie?" Ki asked. "Because I don't."

"No," Jessie replied as she shook her head. "And

I hate to have to do all the shooting we're likely to have ahead of us. But Pleas Barstow's bound to be someplace close by at this time of day. I'm counting on him to try stalling us, trying to get us off guard. If he does, I'll put a few bullets into the ground between his boot toes."

"And if he doesn't stop?" Wright asked.

"I'm betting that he won't," Jessie said. "He's not going to change his ways at all."

"No," Ki agreed. "And I don't think there's much use if we try to figure out much of what we'll be able to do from that point. Do you, Jessie?"

"No," she replied, shaking her head. Then, her voice reflecting fresh determination, she continued. "But as our last resort, hot lead should give the squatters—including Barstow—a message they can understand. So let's stop talking and start moving."

Ki slapped the reins on the rumps of the wagon horse and they all started up the long slope again. By the time they'd gone more than half the distance to the center of the round shallow valley, Jessie had angled her horse several yards away from Ki, and on the other side of the wagon Wright had guided his mount in the opposite direction. They moved slowly up the gentle slope, saving their horses from tiring before there was any real need to whip them up to a faster gait.

Only a short time was needed for them to reach the crest of the rise. Now they could see the entire bowl of the valley. Except for the blackened area where the big tent had been spread when it burned, the valley's floor looked just as it had before the fire occurred.

There seemed to be about the same number of idlers moving about. Women were busy in front of most of the dozen or so small stoves that had been placed beside the tents, and the rope corral at one end of the big depression in the ground contained about the same the number of horses.

When Jessie reined in, Ki followed suit, as did Wright. After they'd taken a quick but thorough look at the valley, Jessie turned to Ki and said, "Suppose you wait here with the wagon and the Gatling gun, Ki. Wright and I will go down and find Barstow and give him warning. If he turns mean and calls out his Galvanized Yankees, I'm sure you'll know what to do to handle the situation."

"I think I will," Ki replied. "We found out a lot about how to handle the gun when we were out on the range shooting it. All I've got to do is crank and put a new can of shells on the ammunition feeding-slot when the one I've been using is empty."

"Well, one thing's for certain," Wright put in. "Likely there won't be any of the Galvanized Yankees trying to get at Ki. I'd guess most of them know what that Gatling gun can do."

"Let's get started, Wright!" Jessie said. "There are more and more of the squatters coming out!

We haven't caught sight of Barstow yet, but he'll have to be getting—"

Jessie broke off and pointed toward a wagon near the charred remains of the tent she and her companions had destroyed. She said, "There's Barstow now! Ki, you stay here. Wright and I need to catch him as soon as we can!"

"Go ahead, then," Ki replied. "I'm sure I've fired the Gatling gun enough to keep it working, so don't worry about me."

Even before Ki had acknowledged her instructions, Jessie was wheeling her horse away. Ed Wright followed her and Ki watched the pair as they rode toward the covered wagon that was Barstow's headquarters. He saw them winding through the dotting of tents and reining in at Barstow's wagon. A few moments after they'd stopped, Barstow emerged.

Jessie toed her mount ahead and reined in as near as possible to Barstow. In a level but determined voice she said, "You know you're asking for more trouble than you can handle. I don't want to have to use that gun to drive your people out of here."

As she was speaking, Jessie turned in her saddle to point to Ki and the wagon that contained the Gatling gun. Ki stood up in the wagon and waved, then jerked its canvas covering away from the weapon.

Even at a distance Ki could see Barstow's jaw drop when, for the first time, he got a look at the burnished brass barrel of the Gatling gun. The squatters' leader turned to Jessie, and Ki could see him waving his arms as he said something to her. She shook her head and gestured again toward Ki.

Now Ki saw that Barstow was continuing to gesticulate at Jessie, his jaw moving up and down rapidly. The distance was too great for Ki to hear anything of the conversation that Barstow and Jessie were having. Ki waited patiently, one hand on the Gatling gun's crank at one side of the weapon's butt, the other hand on the back of the gun barrel.

Then he kneeled beside the weapon and lifted one of the round ammunition feeders into place. He pushed down the small side-lever that locked the drum and barrel together.

He'd already swiveled the barrel of the Gatling gun to aim at the big stretch of burned and heat-stiffened canvas that was all that was left of the big tent. He saw Jessie turn away from Barstow and lift her arm with the muzzle of her rifle pointing to the sky. Ki waited only long enough for the shot she loosed before tightening his grip on the gun's crank.

Ki's use of the Gatling gun had been the subject of a long discussion the evening before, at a confab held by him and Jessie and Wright. Jessie had been adamant about one thing during their discussion: that no shots be fired at or even near any of the squatters.

"We're not going there to kill anybody," she'd said firmly. "All we want to do is to convince them that I don't propose to let them build their new town on Circle Star land. We don't want to have to shoot anybody."

"I suppose not shooting anybody includes Pleas Barstow?" Wright had asked.

"Not even Barstow," Jessie had replied. "He might be especially important to us because the squatters are used to having him as their leader. If we can't get him to persuade them to move peacefully, we'll have to find another way, but it won't be one that includes murder."

"I got to admit I'm glad to hear you say that, Jessie," Wright had replied. "And I got a pretty good idea that Ki is, too."

"It's about what I expected," Ki had told Wright. "And now that the question's been asked and answered, let's see how lucky we are tomorrow, when we get busy with the business at hand."

★

Chapter 14

Crouched in the bed of the wagon with his hand on the Gatling gun's firing crank, Ki had waited patiently for Jessie to finish her long conversation with Barstow. Now, when he got the signal from her shot, he began turning the crank. He'd fired the weapon enough on the previous day to be familiar with its range, and his target was the expanse of charred canvas that still covered a sizable portion of the ground.

There were no tents or bedrolls between him and the big spread of charred tough cloth remaining from the fallen tent that required Ki to be careful. He braced himself as the Gatling gun's bullets lifted an almost unbroken line of dust-puffs and dirt-pocks before the first rounds reached the outspread canvas.

Then, as the bullets began hitting the thick tough fabric, a line of bumps rose in the wake of the slugs, and a dark trail of blotches appeared at the point where the earth had been thrown upward by the bullets.

Ki saw the blotches and began to fan the gun's muzzle, creating a zigzag line in the mixed surface of ashes and dark soil and wrinkled fabric remaining from the tent. He swung the muzzle from side to side, then for a moment moved the gun barrel up and down in short stretches. He did not hear the shouts of anger from the squatters, nor did he stop crisscrossing ragged lines in the fabric until the stream of bullets from the Gatling gun's muzzle came to an abrupt stop.

For a moment Ki gazed at his handiwork. Then he leaped to his feet to remove the empty magazine drum and lift a fresh drum into place. As he worked the screams and shouts from the squatters reached his ears and Ki glanced around. He saw that most of the squatters had stopped, only a few of them still running toward the edge of the big shallow depression. Then he saw Jessie running toward him.

"Stop firing, Ki!" she called. "Barstow's given up! That Gatling gun's been worth a lot more than its weight in gold! Barstow's promised me that he'll pack up and move his squatters away just as quickly as they can get ready to travel!"

Ki's ears had been so close to the rattle of

gunfire from the Gatling gun that he'd heard
Jessie's words only faintly. When he at last
understood what she'd said, Ki rose to his feet
slowly and began looking around. At first he did
not quite believe what he saw.

Not only the squatters, but their horses as well
had reacted to the unending rattle of gunfire.
Most of the animals had been tethered near
their owners' tents. The raucous, unfamiliar
chatter of the weapon had set many of the
animals to neighing and snorting and bucking.
Some of them had fought their tethering stakes
so furiously that they'd managed to pull the stakes
from the ground. Once they'd discovered that they
were free to run, the horses had started to gallop
wildly across the ground. As though to add to the
confusion, a sizable number of the squatters were
running as erratically as the horses when they set
out to catch the animals.

After the Gatling gun's first short volley, the
silence that it had shattered did not return.
Shouts now rose from some of the improvised
shelters, and as Ki turned he saw a handful of
what must have been the Galvanized Yankees
beyond Barstow's tent. They were scattered, but
the distance between them and the tent was
rapidly diminishing.

Ki could see that most of them either carried
rifles or were waving pistols in their hands.
Stepping to his place at the Gatling gun, Ki
swiveled it to bear on the ground a few yards

ahead of the running men and began turning the crank again. The slugs from the weapon raised spurts of earth, and the running men stopped for only a second or two before turning to run in the opposite direction.

Ki stopped firing again. Turning his attention back to Jessie, he saw that Barstow had emerged from it and stepped closer to her. He was gesticulating in a small frenzy of arm-waving, but when Ki saw Jessie's lips moving he also saw Barstow dropping his arms to his sides. Then Barstow nodded to Jessie and again Ki saw her lips moving.

Now Barstow turned and Ki could hear his raised voice faintly, not loudly enough for his words to be distinguished. The Galvanized Yankees had not moved far, and one by one they started drifting back toward the spot where Jessie stood facing Barstow.

By this time the Galvanized Yankees had returned to stand in a small group around Jessie and Barstow. After a few moments had passed, two or three of them them began waving their arms, but Barstow motioned for them to be silent. After they'd listened to him for a few moments, they turned and walked slowly away, scattering as they departed.

Ki finally reached Jessie just as Barstow started to turn and move away from her. Jessie put her forefinger across her lips and Ki nodded. As soon as Barstow was out of earshot, Jessie said, "We've won, Ki. Barstow's taking his squatters some-where else to settle. He's promised to be gone from here before sunset tomorrow."

"And you're sure he won't come back?" Ki asked.

"I'm positive he won't," she replied. "I've told him we're going to keep the Gatling gun here, and assured him that we'll be ready to use it if he does. Now we can get busy with the market herd and go on with our regular business without worrying about him or his Galvanized Yankees."

Turn the page for a sneak preview of a magnificent
new epic series:

RIVERBOAT
by Douglas Hirt

In the golden age of the Mississippi,
men and women from all walks of life
climbed aboard the mighty riverboats
and forged their dreams on the great river,
claiming their destiny in the heart of America.

Look for this new series
starting in March 1995
and coming to you from Jove Books

The thunder rumbled down the streets of Napoleon like cannonfire, rattling windows, startling mules, driving curious faces back from the black and streaked windowpanes. Lightning ripped across the night sky while rain battered the buildings and turned the streets to gumbo. Through it all, Dexter McKay plunged on, a carpetbag and a walking stick wedged under his elbow, jacket clutched closed with one hand, top hat held firmly in place with the other.

Finding a haven from the storm, he halted on the boardwalk beneath a balcony and peered out at the downpour that pounded the tin roof overhead like exploding grapeshot and cascaded in solid opaque sheets, turning streets into flowing rivers.

The sidewalk ended at the tips of his muddy square-toed boots. He squinted through the unrelenting torrents at the vague outline of the sidewalk across the street where another balcony offered a bit of shelter that continued on in a haphazard fashion all the way to the river.

McKay frowned and shook the sleeve of his frock coat, which was already considerably heavier than when he had left the hotel. His fine beaver hat was drenched and limp. He extracted a gold watch from his vest pocket at the very moment a fork of electricity stabbed the earth, illuminating the white dial and gold hands. Thunder rolled through the streets again. He impatiently shoved the watch back into his pocket. He was already wet, so another drenching wouldn't make that much difference.

Top hat firmly clasped, McKay dashed down the two steps to the street, waded through ankle-deep mud, and leaped to the protection of the next boardwalk where he paused to take a breath and to shake himself like a wet dog. Then he was on his way once more, picking up his pace.

At the last building, McKay stopped again and patted dry his eyes, mustache, and small, pointed beard with a silk handkerchief, his eyes straining through the curtain of water. Though no more than half-a-hundred rods off now, he was only barely able to discern the bulky outline of the wharf boat moored at the end of the pier. Beyond it sat the ghostly shapes of two tall side-wheelers, one moment snatched from the darkness and driving rain and the next thrust back again. The river itself had faded completely behind the slanting black shroud. Lights burned upon the two boats there, and on the wharf boat as well. Above the tall stacks of one of the steamboats, cinders sprouted like Fourth of July fountains. Its furnaces were being stoked, and its boilers were building up a head of steam.

Was the pilot actually considering putting out in this weather after all? McKay wondered.

He glanced at the doorway of a saloon he had come to stop by. Past the windowpanes was a bar, mostly empty, and a scattering of tables around an inviting stove, but here and there men clustered about. His eyes moved unerringly toward the card game in progress. *Ah,* he thought, *if I only had the time.* His pocket was woefully light of late because of certain financial setbacks—and a feisty gal by the name of Martha Jo. An hour spent here would certainly correct that deficiency, but, he reminded himself, bigger fish waited to be hooked. He had little to gain holing up here until the storm subsided, and much to be lost, McKay mused, grinning to himself.

Just then he heard the steamboat's whistle give two short shrills.

It was departing!

McKay dashed out into the deluge and dove headlong along the wooden pier and onto the wharf boat, which had been built upon the derelict hull of an old steamer and still wore a promenade running completely around the upper deck. He ducked under it, out of the rain, jogging around the other side to where the *Natchez* was docked— rather *had* been docked!

He arrived in time to see the foam churning beneath her paddle wheels, showing her stern light to the wharf.

"Damnation!" McKay shouted, dropping his carpetbag. His arms flagged furiously at the *Natchez*, but she ignored him and faded into the stormy night. For a moment only the red glow of her open fireboxes lingered, and then that, too, was gone. The pounding of her engines was lost in the roar of the rain, and McKay stood there, momentarily at a loss and becoming thoroughly drenched.

He picked up the bag and stepped into the wharf boat, shook himself off, found a bench in the empty waiting room, and flopped down upon it to think. An old Negro pushing a broom across the way eyed McKay curiously, keeping his head down.

"That was the steamboat *Natchez* that just departed, was it not?"

"Suh?" The Negro came half out of a stoop, seemingly unable to straighten up any further.

"The steamboat that just pulled out. Was it the *Natchez*?"

"Yes, suh. Him is de *Natchez*."

"Figured as much. And there goes my game as well. You know who was aboard?"

"No, suh."

"Devol, that's who!"

The Negro looked at him blankly.

"Well, never mind. It wouldn't make any difference to you, anyway, I suppose."

The black man went back to his sweeping.

McKay looked down at himself, made a face, and proceeded to squeeze water from his sleeve into a growing puddle at his feet. "You wouldn't happen to have a towel somewhere around here?"

"Yes, suh." The Negro set aside his broom and returned with a thin cotton cloth.

"Thank you." McKay shed his frock coat and wrung it out outside beneath the promenade, and dried himself as best he could. A stove in the corner drove the chill from the damp air. He wiped his shoes, then the puddle around his feet, and stood for a while in front of the stove as the lightning flashed upon the window and the thunder shook the wharf boat. Through the foggy glass McKay could see the other steamboat moored beyond. He cleared the glass with his sleeve, but the name on her paddle box was obscured by a pile of cargo waiting on the dock to be loaded.

The black man had finished his task and was making his way down the hallway when McKay asked, "What boat is that?"

He turned back, peered at the window where McKay was jabbing a thumb, and said, "Him be de TEMPEST QUEEN, suh."

"The TEMPEST QUEEN? Bound upriver or down?"

"I don't know dat, suh."

McKay frowned. "Well, it hardly makes any difference now." He was disgusted with himself for having lingered so long at the hotel—just the same, he had to grin in spite of it all, remembering what had kept him. She had taken his last dollar, true, but then some things are well worth the price.

"Thank you anyway," he said, and the Negro disappeared as McKay rotated himself in front of the stove like a pig roasting on a spit while the wharf boat pitched upon the back of the angry, swollen river. Shortly his clothes began to steam, and the warmth worked its way into his body.

Now that the steamboat *Natchez* had departed without him, he studied on his next move. He considered returning to the hotel and Martha Jo, but the bottom of his pockets held only lint, a crumpled handkerchief, and a worthless, soggy steamboat ticket. McKay knew well enough it wasn't his good looks that had attracted the pretty tart's attentions. Ah, well, there was always that card game back at the saloon. The briefest of grins came to his face, followed by another frown. McKay had no desire to dive back into this Arkansas storm.

He glanced out the streaming window at the white, three-tiered "wedding cake" moored there and wondered again where she was bound, then put that thought out of mind. The *Natchez* was the fastest boat on the river, and this one would have no hope of catching her—even if she were ready to depart. The erratic streaks of lightning showed only the faintest wisps of black smoke above her stacks. She was not preparing to shove off anytime soon.

McKay's fist clenched as he thought of the opportunity missed. Devol was the most celebrated gambler on the Mississippi, and where he went, high-stakes rollers followed. Enough for an ambitious gent such as himself to siphon off a couple marks for a bit of fleecing of his own.

And it was his own fault—well, mostly. As he stood there drying himself out, he became aware of the voices drifting down the hallway, the muffled laughter, an occasional moan or shout of elation. McKay's mood was not such as he wanted company tonight. To be alone with his thoughts and to pull together a fresh plan were all McKay wanted. Perhaps he could find another steamer and catch up with the action farther down the river.

His glance went back to the riverboat outside, and a germ of a plan began to form.

Presently he grew aware of a new sound emanating from the hallway, and his full attention was at once riveted—as a prima donna's attention is galvanized at the opening bars of the orchestra or a factory worker at the whistle of a shift change. McKay listened again.

Yes, he was certain now. It was the click of coins being gathered up.

He thrust his hand into his pocket and came out with a soggy lint ball, but Dexter McKay was smiling anyway as he abandoned the comfortable warmth of the stove and grabbed up his valise and frock coat.

Along either side of the hallway down the middle of the wharf boat was an assortment of rooms: offices, storage rooms, waiting room, and finally, the gentlemen's card room. The door was open, and beyond it six or seven men stood around watching the game in progress at the table. McKay stepped inside and nodded to the men standing about, but no one paid him much attention—except the gentleman in control of the cards at the table. He looked quickly over, measured McKay at a glance, and returned his attention to the cards he was shuffling about on the tabletop, but not before McKay caught the fleeting look of concern—or was it irritation?—in the man's eyes.

Across the table was an older fellow clothed in a blue box-cut jacket decorated in gold braid, with a star on the cuff. He was wearing a dark blue billed cap, likewise emblazoned in gold, pushed back on top of his head. He sported a gray beard, trimmed close to the face, and crow's-feet radiating out from his blue eyes, appearing deeper now by the intense scowl that had settled there.

McKay positioned himself next to the stove and

draped his coat over his ebony walking stick near to it as he watched the game.

The fellow in control of the cards gave a short, friendly laugh and said, "We will try it one more time. I think you finally got the hang of it, Captain Hamilton."

The other man, whom McKay had already figured out was a riverboat captain, and most probably the master of the very steamer presently moored to the wharf boat, gave a short grunt. He was not so convinced.

The gambler laid out the cards. McKay coughed into his sleeve to hide the grin that emerged. They were playing his game. Three-card monte, and he recognized the pitch he had just heard as something he'd said perhaps no less than a thousand times before, to as many unwary souls who were about to give up the game in despair before they lost their last nickel as well as their watch and cuff links.

"One more try," the captain said, "then we play a real card game, not this fancy shuffle-and-guess gambit."

The gambler smiled as if his lips had been well oiled. "You're a shrewd opponent, Captain Hamilton. You sit there and place small bets until you have me figured out, and then you move in for the kill. I wonder if I shouldn't pull out while I am ahead?" He laughed.

'Twas a good line, McKay thought. He made a mental note to add it to his own repertoire.

The captain only barely managed to hide his own small smile. The man was hooked. McKay recognized the signs.

Another furtive glance at the doorway—then back at the cards now turned faceup on the table, and the dealer said, "Your choice, sir."

The captain leaned forward and squinted at the pictures on the three cards—a man, a lady, and a baby. "The lady," he said, pushing two gold coins across. The gambler matched his bet.

The man and baby cards were turned over, and finally the lady card. Back and forth they slid upon the tabletop. McKay was only mildly impressed with the man's dexterity. He had seen better. Certainly he himself was more the master of the cards than this man. The gambler played it straight—as McKay would have done at this point to keep the captain interested.

Captain Hamilton studied the cards when they had come finally to rest in a line.

"That one," he said, turning over an end card. The lady!

The gambler fixed a most pained expression to his face and gave a long, heartfelt sigh of resignation. "You certainly have my mark, sir."

Captain Hamilton laughed and hauled over the pile of coins to his side of the table.

Very nice. Now raise the stakes some.

The gambler turned the cards faceup again and said, "You bested me that time, Captain. I wonder if my luck ain't all used up."

174

"One more time, Mr. Banning," Captain Hamilton said.

The gambler frowned and said dismally, "I don't know, Captain. I suspect I shall regret this in the morning," and, as if to fortify his waning courage, he took a long sip from the glass of whiskey at his elbow and sleeved his lips dry. "Well, all right then, I shall go one more round."

The captain was delighted and worked his fingers across his palm as if he'd suddenly developed an itch. The gambler looked vaguely concerned, and McKay didn't think the expression was wholly for Captain Hamilton's benefit as Banning cast another surreptitious peek out the doorway.

Captain Hamilton selected the lady card again, commenting that she had turned lucky for him, and beyond that, McKay caught the gleam in Captain Hamilton's eye, for the captain, too, had discerned the smallest of a coffee stain or some such mark on the back of that particular card.

Money bet, cards turned over, the gambler shuffled them about and straightened them into a line with a slender forefinger.

McKay smirked.

The captain bent over, stroking his gray beard, considering. But he was poor at hiding the spark of victory that brightened his face. And now the gambler, as if unaware of the other man's advantage, cleared his throat and said innocently, "I may just raise this here bit, sir, if it pleases you, as I see you are in a quandary." That was a flat lie.

McKay coughed into his sleeve again.

The captain, who already had the winning card spied, leaped at this offer, although he tried—and not very successfully—to hide his delight behind a stern face.

"How much?"

The gambler considered a moment, chewing a corner of his lips, and said, "Fifty dollars?"

"Done!" Captain Hamilton thrust a fist into a pocket of his blue coat and tossed the appropriate coins onto the pile. The gambler added his money and said, "Turn over your pick, sir."

Hamilton turned over the marked card. He was stunned. It was the baby. "What's this!" he bellowed.

Some of the men standing about sniggered.

In an instant, Captain Hamilton flipped over the remaining cards. The man and the lady were there, as they should have been.

"But I—" he began to say and then realized he'd been suckered, and he was too embarrassed to pursue the matter any further with so many men about.

McKay, of course, was not at all surprised, for he, and only he, had seen the original marked card slip into the gambler's sleeve at the very instant the replacement—identically marked—had slid out and taken its place.

Hamilton's neck glowed crimson, and to regain

face he said, "Enough of this. No more fancy shifting of the cards. I'll have my money back, and I'll do it fair."

"Name your game, sir," Banning said easily.

"Old sledge," Hamilton replied.

The gambler agreed and played it smooth, but McKay wondered about the man's keen interest in the doorway, although no one else in the room seemed to have noticed. One of the men tossed another scoop of coal into the stove, and by this time McKay's coat had ceased steaming and he shrugged back into the still-damp apparel, although it was quite warm and toasty now. He leaned his weight on his walking stick and studied the careful manner in which the gambler returned his monte cards to an inside pocket of his saffron sack coat and retrieved a fresh pack of cards from somewhere else within it.

"I got my own cards," Captain Hamilton said, quickly adding to temper the accusation in the tone of his voice, "not that I don't trust yours, sir."

"Of course," Banning said, his slippery smile sliding across his face. "Your cards are acceptable."

At that moment, a woman appeared at the doorway. She paused a moment to shake out a dripping umbrella and then, smiling coyly as if surprised to discover the room filled with rough men who had suddenly discovered her standing there, said, "Excuse me, but I am looking for my uncle, Mr. Theodore de Winter." She glanced around at each of their faces and, discovering that her uncle was not among them, said, "Oh, dear. I was supposed to meet him here, on the wharf boat, tonight."

A man in greasy overalls—an engineer or striker by appearance—said, "I don't know the name."

She said, somewhat dismayed, "He is Colonel Matthew de Winter's brother. The colonel is my father."

She spoke in a lovely drawling Southern cadence that was music to McKay's ears. He'd been away from proper society too many years, he decided, drinking in the charm of her perfect face, her sparkling eyes. Her cheeks were somewhat flushed, her eyes very blue and wide, her complexion was what McKay was certain, in the South, would qualify as "peaches and cream."

The name de Winter didn't mean anything to the men in the room—and it certainly didn't mean anything to McKay, who had only recently arrived from the booming tent city along Cherry Creek, in the Kansas Territory, where the cry of *"Gold!"* had flooded the once-peaceful land at the base of the Rocky Mountains with thousands of prospectors.

"Perhaps he has been delayed," she said hopefully.

"Maybe he left on the *Natchez,*" said a stoutly-built man to McKay's left. He wore the rough clothes of a dock worker or stevedore and had muscles enough for such employment. The man continued. "She just pulled out, not half an hour ago."

"Oh, that's impossible. Uncle Theodore would not have left without me, and besides we had not booked passage on the *Natchez*."

She shivered then in a draft coming down the hallway, and McKay instantly doffed his hat and was immediately at her side. "Miss de Winter. I see you are chilled. Please take my place by the stove," he said, taking her by the arm despite her ever-so-slight protest.

"Well, all right, for a moment," she agreed.

Someone else in the room said, "You just stay as long as you like, missy. Your uncle will show up directly." There was at once universal agreement on this as the men stood and sat a bit straighter now, and their aim at the cuspidors improved some as well.

"My name is Dexter McKay," he said and bowed slightly at his waist. He pulled a card from his vest and pencil from his pocket and scrawled *At your service!* beneath his name and handed it to the lovely woman.

"Genevieve de Winter," she replied, smiling sweetly. She took the card, glanced at it, and put it into her handbag. "You speak like a Northerner, sir."

"Ohio."

"Oh." She only partly hid her disapproval. "I

declare, I have never been farther north than St. Louis, although my father, the colonel, has traveled most all over the world."

"Really?"

"He is touring Spain and Portugal at this very moment."

"And your uncle is chaperoning while he is away?"

"Of course," she said most properly.

Banning took a cigar from an inside pocket, put a match to it, and offered one to Captain Hamilton. The captain declined.

The game began.

Banning had taken no notice of Genevieve de Winter. The captain had offered only a passing interest when she had entered the room. The cut gave Banning first deal. Hamilton's full attention was now on six cards he'd picked up off the table. The men looking on had their attentions divided, but after the game commenced, their eyes mostly remained on the two men facing each other across the table.

Genevieve craned her neck slightly to see the action, more than just a little curious.

McKay's interest was professional. He wondered what kind of gambler Banning really was. He had already figured out Captain Hamilton and decided that if the captain ran his boat the way he played cards, then passage aboard her would be a dangerous excursion indeed. The man had *the disease,* and he was an easy mark. He was an honest and open fellow, and his eyes at once either frowned or beamed when he gathered up his hand. He might just as well spread it out on the tabletop for all to see.

Banning, on the other hand, was a professional. Perhaps not as good as himself, McKay decided, but quite competent nonetheless. Just the same, he seemed to be doing exceptionally well.

An hour passed. Captain Hamilton was out a little over twelve hundred dollars by McKay's reckoning and more determined than ever to win it all back—even if it took all night and every dollar in his pocket to do so.

The men in the room forgot Genevieve de Winter, their attention engrossed by Hamilton's spectacular losses as the cards went round the table again and again. McKay discovered that Banning no longer seemed concerned with the doorway, and just as odd, he seemed always to know exactly what cards Hamilton was holding, making no effort to soften the blows he had been dealing to the captain's purse.

With Genevieve de Winter forgotten—and how that could be was a deep mystery to McKay— their postures took the path of least resistance, and the cuspidors once again were safe from the continual streams of brown tobacco juice squirted in their direction.

McKay, however, the consummate student of human nature that he was, had not forgotten her, and now his curiosity went beyond the pale peach color of her crêpe de chine flounces, flowing in layers over the steel hoops of her crinoline, and the white belled sleeves and ruffled cuffs of her shirtwaist, or the elaborately decorated straw bonnet upon her head. His eyes kept returning to the folded umbrella in her hands and the curious way it shifted slightly every so often. It took McKay but a few minutes of careful observation to discern the pattern.

Well, well, Banning was working with a capper—and a lovely accomplice she was. His admiration for the woman swelled. They were fleecing the captain admirably, and it really wasn't business after all. Now that he had the game figured out, it was easy to catch Banning slipping a card up a sleeve for dealing a second or slowly moving the edge of the top card over the shiny, flat-topped gold ring Banning wore on his little finger, turned around and facing up now.

McKay was suddenly thinking of the famous Devol aboard the *Natchez*, his own opportunities missed, and the woeful state of his finances at the moment. He had used most of his ready cash to buy the now-worthless steamboat ticket, and the rest of it—well, he tried not to think of that, for he was endeavoring to concentrate on the moves Banning was using. He marveled at how blind everyone else in the room was to them.

If he could somehow find passage down the

river, he might catch up with Devol and company. . . . Just then an idea took root and then bloomed, like a brilliant tulip in spring, and he could hardly restrain the grin that wanted out this time.

If you enjoyed this book, subscribe now and get...

TWO FREE

A $7.00 VALUE—